SPLINTER SALEM

PART 1

BEWARE

BELIEVE

A SPACE FABLE by WAYNE HILL

Splinter Salem Part One

Splinter Salem, Volume 1

Wayne Hill

Published by Wayne Hill, 2021.

SPLINTER SALEM PART ONE

First edition. December 1, 2021.

Copyright © 2021 Wayne Hill.

ISBN: 978-1393038252

Written by Wayne Hill.

FOR TOMMY & MARIE

Author: Wayne Hill

Artwork: Wayne Hill

Copy Editors: Derek Hill

Marie Casey

PART 1
PROLOGUE:
First Contact

When the first humans reached Australia About 45,000 years ago, they quickly drove to extinction 90% of its large animals. This was the first significant impact that Homo sapiens had on Earths ecosystem. It was not the last.
-YUVAL NOAH HARARI

PROLOGUE

Five minutes, thirty-eight seconds, and seven split seconds post-arrival of deep space exploration craft Neptune to Gliese 581d, the age-old question of whether we are alone in the universe finally had a resolute answer.

The aliens were nicknamed Buckies by an over enthusiastic zoologist, who noted a certain similarity in the shell shape of the aliens to that of the whelk, whose Latin name was *Buccinum undatum*. Their scale, however, was significantly different. Buckies were three to four times the size of Earth's blue whales, highly intelligent, friendly, herbivorous, and aesthetically unpleasant. (Actually, to say that Buckies are aesthetically unpleasant is a perverse understatement, the greatest fantasy of the millennium. It is like saying Pluto is a bit nippy in winter! The foul appearance of these highly unusual alien creatures could stop you dead in your tracks and cause you to evacuate your bowels.) Hundreds of first encounters with these mysterious and terrifying creatures has unwittingly ended many a brave explorer's intention of visiting other planets, and, indeed, meeting anything with more eyes than themselves.

Buckies have a head superficially like that exhibited by Earth's terrestrial snails, but it has two bulbous, stalk-less and glowing eyes either side of what appears to be a demonically horned skull mask. Affix a bone-white demon mask to a whelk and grow it in size two million times and you can better picture a Buckie. Housed inside a Buckies' mask is a curled-up tentacle, which due to convergent evolution is not entirely dissimilar to the molluscan radula. Outwardly, the eyes of Buckies look like the compound eyes of Earth flies, in part, anyway. Most of the bulk of Buckies is composed of hard shell and soft, slug-like flesh.

The Buckies had no comprehension of why the strange visitors had come to their peaceful planet. Their unpolluted ecosystem and delicate habitat — the product of millions of years of evolution — changed within Earth-weeks of the humans' arrival, and within fifty Earth-years there were major issues. The humans knew that the creatures had no idea of the term 'overcrowding,' no understanding of the motives of the United Space Association (USA). The innocent — or perhaps, naïve — Buckies saw no threat to their world or way of life. They observed these peculiar human visitors as a source of interest, in a child-like way.

Buckies went about their silent existence in the deep ocean canyons, buried in the sludge they generate by eating the diverse marine plant life of the planet. The curious beasts lived centred around bubbling hydrothermal vents, channels to the planet's life-giving core, only surfacing occasionally to feed on plankton and the planet's abundant algae-like lifeforms. Those who first observed the colossal aliens in a herd on the sea floor, churning the ocean's sediment, believed that the world was in flux, the mantle shifting with an unnaturally rapid geologic speed.

One Earth-year after the arrival of humans, most of the Buckies had been wiped out. Humans dramatically altered the oceanic temperatures as they began their terraforming to extend the habitable zone of the planet. They triggered eruptions from the core of the planet, as enhanced volcanic action was a necessity to produce land mass. The Buckies could do nothing but swim, leviathan-like, to the darker, colder side of the planet. Gliese 581d had a furnace-side, tidally-locked to face the gaze of its star, Gliese, and a dark-side, where the temperatures were the exact opposite — a fierce cold, unimaginable to most humans.

Over the following five centuries the population of these majestic creatures had diminished so dramatically it seemed extinction was inevitable. Humans took several male and female samples and kept them contained and safe until the terraforming was complete. The Buckies were then reintroduced into designated areas of the planet, protected in reservations, and they seemed to settle well and thrive. Their collective misery for lost family and friends remained as buried as their secret lives under the vast ocean before the arrival of their human overlords.

The science fiction books of Earth's long-lost past told numerous stories of human-like aliens. Aliens with similar intelligence and inhabiting the same conscious plane of thought as Earthlings: similar wants and materialistic needs ... and the same desire to kill all those deemed inferior to themselves. These fictitious aliens all existed in the same dimension, the same reality.

Humans are the tentacle-horrors from Mars — of early 50s movies — wantonly dispatching death as soon as they see alternative life. We are the evil aliens, with lasers for eyes, that did *not* come in peace.

Humanity ventured to many more planets after Gliese 581d, but no matter how many worlds they visited, everything followed the same pattern. It came as no shock, after a few more millennia had elapsed, that no creature encountered

could match *Homo sapiens* when it came to invention, forethought, or ruthless competitive survival instincts.

Humans had innumerable dreams of the future they intended to carve into the heavens above them: what strange and fascinatingly intelligent lifeforms they could meet to better their knowledge of the universe. Unfortunately, the lifeforms discovered by Earth's brave adventurers served only to fuel a deep despair within Man. There was a question that burned solar flare-bright in the minds of early space adventurers: are we the only race that has left their home-world? Are we the only space-faring species?

In the centuries that have elapsed since the discovery of Buckies, aliens were discovered on many habitable planets in the Milky Way and neighbouring Andromeda galaxy. All these alien species had an intellectual capacity akin to that of many Earth mammals: cows, dogs, pigs, and dolphins. Our collective ego revelled in this discovery and proclaimed that humans, as the only lifeform discovered to have left their planet of origin, are the supreme universal intelligence. We named ourselves gods.

The first alien race known to humans, Buckies, were found to have many alien compounds inside them that proved beneficial to humans. They became cattle, farmed and harvested for health and beauty products. Consequently, the aliens of other worlds became nothing more than food — food for the self-declared gods of space, an intergalactic smorgasbord of unusual flavours.

CHAPTER ONE

The Facility

> Life isn't about finding yourself.
> Life is about creating yourself.
>
> - George Bernard Shaw -

1

Inside the small grey room, a young boy cradles his bandaged blood-stained arm. He occasionally removes his injured right arm from the comfort of his still-healing midsection, chancing a look. His eyes narrow as he peeks under the sticky bandage, brow marked with concern. Underneath the raised incisions on his forearm, light radiates — the soft and warm pastel tones mock his pain.

"Join, why don't you join?"

The boy whispers to his injured arm and the lights, he whispers to the advanced biotech buried deep in his muscle mass. Hoping, praying that something far beyond the boundaries of Scientific Reason might be listening, that something might obey his will.

A knock on the door makes him jump. He pulls down the sleeve of his jacket to cover his arm, revealing the silver and red emblem of The USA's Diamond Lights School for the Gifted. Blood soaks into the sleeve — the silver emblem now looking less than majestic, patchy with the blood of the innocent.

A middle-aged woman clad in white robes carries a silver tray. The tray has on it a syringe-gun and two small vials of golden liquid.

"Here. Both our formulas," the woman cheerfully announces as she presents the tray.

The boy looks at the metal tray and then the woman.

"No thanks," says the boy, through gritted teeth, as he turns his attention back to his arm.

"Tommy, please take your formula. I'll take mine. We can optimise, and talk."

"Mary, just take both, and tell everyone I've taken mine. Go optimal, keep a level of sanity around this asylum, and — hell, I don't know! — just keep it secret."

"No. Not again, Tommy. We'll get in trouble, maybe banished if the Believers find out."

"I don't care. I'm not taking that formula anymore."

"Why not?"

"Because I know what it is."

"And what, exactly, is it?"

"Apathy in a tube. Contentment in a container. All your dreams come true; all your dreams to dust."

"What does that mean?" asks Mary, as she takes a shot of golden liquid to the neck. The golden liquid shines for a while under the skin — it spreads out like a web across her neck, and then vanishes. "It's just formula," she says.

He stares at her.

"Everyone takes it," she adds.

"Well, everyone needs to start trying something else, because this is insane. Optimising and going Optimal is pointless if your brain thinks the same as other brains. Just gaining knowledge to know things, where's the greatness in that?" asks Tommy.

"The things you did today need addressing. That poor teacher. You're taking the work detail from The Association too far. The work you have done for them is quite enough. We need you to concentrate on Drumcroon matters, not Associate matters."

"No, I feel as if you deserve some insight into my plans because you see me as something I'm not, and it's bothering me. I'm not doing either of the things you mentioned. Although, on the surface, I can see where your Optimal thoughts are being generated. That's what it looks like. It's one or the other with all you formula fans, isn't it, Mary?

No, I'm not doing either. I'm using the Drumcroon facility only to eat, sleep and shit in. I'm using The Association for access to equipment I wouldn't normally be permitted to use," says Tommy, clutching his arm.

"How is it?" asks the woman with concern, looking at Tommy's arm.

"Well, Mary, it's not great," says Tommy, sarcastically. He pulls up his sleeve to show her a mutilated arm with wires and less-than-perfect stitches holding down swelling implants. Blood abounds.

"You've gone too far this time, Tommy!" Mary's hand has come up and is covering her mouth.

"Nope, this is just the beginning. If these implants take, that is. I have three more procedures and then I should be finished."

"Has your father seen this?"

"No. I think he walked past me once while I was cleaning the floor in the circle room. That was two weeks ago."

"He's a busy man. He has this place to run, and the Believers and the Association hold him accountable for just about everything."

"I know. I'd like to say I understand, but I don't. We are different people, I suppose."

"Looks sore ... Is it?" asks Mary.

Tommy shrugs. "The pain comes in waves. The first set of implants, last fall, damaged my nerve endings. I don't feel much in this arm. Anyway, thanks for the concern, but you're worrying about things that are beyond your mental reach. Your Optimal capabilities are useless here, so it's pointless."

"You're doing odd things to yourself, Tommy, but — if this is what makes you happy — I suppose you know best. Please, for me, take this formula. I don't want to lose you to this place. Wild animals roam the woods, and you know, if you get yourself banished, you're just going to be food for the bears."

"I'm not worried about bears," Tommy says holding up his injured arm.

"Come on, Tommy, for me," says Mary, holding the tray out towards him, the formula shimmering in the light.

"I've told you; it doesn't work on me. It would be a waste of formula. I have immunity to the formula. I made myself a serum which I took for three months. It contains psilocybin, Lion's Mane, Ginko Biloba, and other such plants. I added a parasitical fungus, called *Cordyceps sinensis*, and after applying a few waves of energy, at the right time, to my brain ... boom! I made myself immune to formula."

"But it's just formula, Tommy! Everybody tak —"

"You know what, Mary?" he interrupts. "I've got some suffering to do here, and you're just giving me more pain of the head and ear variety. Please can you go. Tell them I've taken it. Please. I'll act reasonably from now on, I swear. I just need a little time to finalise some things I've been working on and then, I promise you, I'll be no trouble at all."

"Well, you know best, I suppose. You always know best. And what am I going to do with this?" She holds up the formula.

"Mary, you do all these calibrations, all these mind-strengthening acts. What are you doing with all this newly

gained wisdom? All this health and ... wealth of mind? What are you creating? Please just leave, I ... am in some pain," says Tommy, through gritted teeth.

Mary looks at the tray, then Tommy.

"Not everybody wants to make things, Tommy."

Tommy cradles his injured arm, tucking it into his stomach, and points to the door with the other arm.

"Thank you," Tommy says.

Mary walks to the door, opens it and, without turning, she quietly says, "I made you." She closes the door behind her, takes Tommy's dose of golden fluid and injects the contents of the gun-syringe into her neck. She winces a little, her pupils dilating within glazed eyes.

She strolls down the long corridor of doors. Doors which lead to rooms with sleeping children. Other Guardians' children: Optimal children. She thinks only clear thoughts, only good things. She's Optimal and focused, going to her next dutiful task.

Back in the small grey room, Tommy is lying on his bed staring into nothingness. He repeats the same line of dialogue, in different languages, as he clasps his mutilated arm tight to his chest. The glowing lumps beneath his skin rise and fall with his tonal inflection, dancing with the pitch of each sentence.

"*Non enim natus es ut ego rogabo.*"

"Lm 'atlub 'an 'akun mkhlwaqana."

"Mi ne petis esti kreita."

"Je n'ai pas demandé à être créé."

"Ich habe nicht darum gebeten, geschaffen zu warden."

"Watashi wa sakusei sa reru koto o motomemasendeshita."

"Ez nuen sortzea eskatu

"Wǒ méiyôu yāoqiú bèi chuàngzào."

"Jeg bad ikke om at blive oprettet."

"Ik heb niet gevraagd om gecreeerd te worden."

"Ég bad ekki um ad vera búinn til."

"Níor iarr mé go gcruthófaí mé."

"Es neprasīju, lai mani izveido."

"Sakusei o irai shinakatta."

"Aš neprašiau būti sukurtas."

"Čhån mì dî khx hî šrāng."

"I didn't ask to be created."

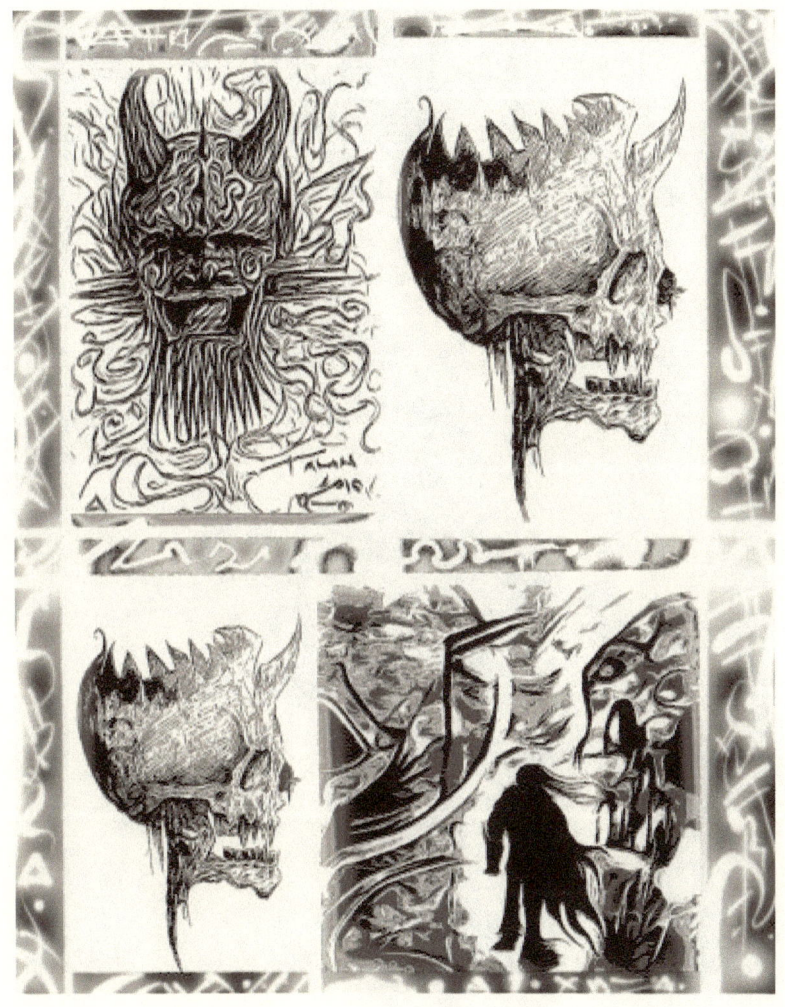

CHAPTER TWO

The Weeping Willow

> We live on a placid island of ignorance
> in the midst of black seas of infinity, and it
> was not meant that we should voyage far.
>
> -H P Lovecraft-

2

Of all the troubling hypotheses and mind-boggling conundrums

that exist in this agreed reality, two quandaries lift their heads high

above any others as giants of arcana: infinity and nothingness. These

two marauding head-scratchers are forever marked as Enigma's

unrewarded champions.

These two subject matters have set many open-ended questions that scientists, philosophers and freethinkers continue to struggle with today. Infinity and nothingness. These two topics have the power to push rational and intellectual faculties to their limit. Infinity and nothingness: perhaps doomed to be opposing twins of mystery, invariably attracting interest within many a scientific, philosophical, and even psychedelic debate since humankind's earliest investigations — whether they be purposeful and directed studies of the physics behind the universe, or the more spiritual paths of hermetic, gnostic, or shamanic pursuits.

Human psychedelic voyagers have rituals that include drugs such as psilocybin, the molecule DMT, Peyote and *Salvia divinorum*. Adventurers' constraints and self-made boundaries of physical and mental capabilities never falter in the way of mankind's deep curiosity to map what cannot be mapped; to recover the missing part of the puzzle, or the rare creature that has eluded the sharpest of minds since the idea of

mind. The traveller ventures forth into the darkest depths for the enrichment of their soul.

When we stare into the abyss — the void of nothingness — or out from it, into the infinite, we will regularly encounter something dwelling there, something set aside that will unsettle, inspire, encourage.

The human philosopher Carl Gustav Jung once stated: 'No tree's branches can reach heaven, except the one whose roots have originated in hell.'

What if there is a person or being in existence who has witnessed infinitude; lived inside nothingness? How would that person survive? Who would they be able to talk to? Some experiences of searching for those hidden answers can lead to chilling conclusions. What is known now by our whiskey-drum minds? We know how to drown unexplainably terrifying thoughts with fermented and distilled goods, forever ensuring a particular agreeableness.

On Earth — where humans still dwell, albeit against their will — there exists a place where all these mysterious wonderings are either nurtured or quenched. A place where the most significant and strangest minds tussle over problems amongst like-minded kin. We know this place as: The Pub.

This pub is unique because it bears the title of 'the last public house on Earth'. This pub is very isolated and this little place for lost souls is kept by Mr and Mrs O'Shea and their only child, Marie-Ann. The patrons of the pub are obliged to abide by only two rules (failure to do so is guaranteed to attract one of Marie-Ann O'Shea's uncompromisingly brutal mood swings):

• Everyone is welcome (with a song in their hearts)

• Bad behaviour will be dealt with (harshly).

The pub goes by the name *The Weeping Willow*. Outside the pub, its namesake, a cascading waterfall of green, is situated only a few metres away, towering at forty feet high, behind a lowly six-foot tall drystone wall. Many of the locals often take time out of their routine to stare at the ancient and majestic tree. The gentle swishing of the tree's delicate, arching branches invokes a sense of tranquillity and peace. They rustle in the breeze: a whisper, a conversation both personal and meaningful to every patron and passer-by. This mighty tree is the last of its kind.

There are many 'last of a kind's on Earth now, as it is made up of only one small island landmass. The only landmass to survive the meteorite impact of 4423 AD (*Anno Domini*). Historical geography of the planet Earth would position the surviving land mass of 9,000 sq. miles as part of the United States of Hampshire America (most of New Hampshire and a part of Maine). A small part (36.5 sq. miles) of the remaining land — the part of New Hampshire was previously known as the county of Rockingham — is the town of Derry, known to the locals as 'Space Town' because it was the birthplace of the first man from the United States to go into space.

The old motto for the state of New Hampshire is *Live free or die*, though considering the way of life today, a more appropriate motto might have been *Live free, die soon*.

The population of the land mass is dictated by the Drumcroon Facility, positioned on the east coast of the island. The population fluctuates at the facility, with the diverse assortment of prisoners originating from many settlements across the universe. The prisoners arrive via a shuttle link to the spaceport orbiting eighty kilometres above Earth.

Earth is a prison planet, as are most planets that have breathable atmospheres or have been terraformed to be habitable (in accordance with USA regulations). It is also essential to mention that no humans of this time would, in their right mind, live out in the open. The only exceptions to this are the prisoners — who have no choice in the matter — and the Guardians monitoring them. The prisoners are more than likely to die within the first three months, as venturing out onto the remains of the island previously known as The Granite State — New Hampshire, West America, Earth — is a death sentence.

Earth is just as dangerous — if not more so — than any other breathable planet in the explored universe, because of increased levels of bacteria, mutated viruses and the slow decay caused by gravity. The primary hazard, however, is overcrowding. Hundreds of people are exiled to prison planet Earth every month and this overpopulation encourages the formation of warring tribes; nomadic existences that are wild and unpredictable. Those born on the prison planet know no other way of life.

The arrival of the newly deposited prisoners is an exhilarating time for the clans' leaders. For the banished individual (depending on their level of usefulness) it signifies either a fresh start with an adopted family or a miserable and transitory existence relying on compassion and charity — both of which are rare commodities on any prison planet.

To the west of the island is the Lanes, a highly prized safe zone. Built by the outcast, the Lanes are strengthened, reworked and repurposed fortifications: a protective measure against undesirable additions to the population. Located beyond a huge, elliptical concrete wall, it is a one-mile wide (fifteen-miles around) band of shanty townhouses. The shape of this area is a bizarre, elongated dartboard: The Weeping Willow pub is the bullseye, the recreational areas are the small single beds, farmland plots stretch from the trebles to the doubles, and — radiating from the doubles to the edge of the board — the residential shanty houses. At one end of the Lanes, behind a fortified, guarded barrier (and a thick sea wall) is the ocean; at the opposite end, the barricade is shattered, and, across an ocean of poison-barbed twisted metal, there is the Barrens.

The Guardians are governed by the Believers, whether they like it or not. The Guardians are powerless to stop the Believers as they robotically enforce the Believers' banishment laws. Groups of people governing groups of people — always in circles; but some circles are bigger than others.

'What benefits humanity?' is the main concern of the Guardians.

'What benefits the Believers?' is the main duty of the Believers.

When the Believers first came to power, they call their banishment of people to prison planets the 'expulsion of evildoers.' This motto hurts the ears and minds of the newly exiled. It eventually mutates into a system for culling the weak from the strong. People within the United Space Association are ruthlessly trying to gain Credits (the USA monetary system) to improve their lifestyle. The Guardians are trying to keep their focus, stay Optimal, and keep humanity moving towards the Guardian's idealised (or channelled) vision of a future not yet understood. Within these three very different societies, two of the societies do not care what happens on Earth. The society on Earth cares only about everything as a whole — the individual prisoner does not matter. The prisoners are the only community dealing with the immediacy of life. They live within a foreign, alien reality, compared with the protected Guardians, in the Drumcroon facility, or the USA, scattered across the universe in their boil-like biodomes. The thoughts of the prisoners, if they survive the first few weeks, are truly free. Banished by the heartless, the prisoners experience life at its most ruthless and savage, but they are alive. Exiles are taken to the Drumcroon facility, or other facilities equally as efficient, like a partially terraformed hellhole in the outer reaches of the Andromeda galaxy; some prison dome, some place, where the lights remain off. The Believers, in their Temples in space, have absolute control — absolute power combined with a self-serving agenda that has no time for the tears of the innocent. When questioned about innocent prisoners, the courts of the Believers say: "There are no innocent people on a prison planet."

The Believers' courts are terrifying places. They surround the criminal in three-dimensional hologram forms, the Believers facing the accused from every angle of the round courtroom. The person on trial usually has their head hanging in shame — they know the outcome before the sentence is passed. The real horror of the Believers' court is the absence of anything resembling a just and humane trial; it is a one-sided affair with only one result: banishment. There are many memory plate recordings of the Believers finding people guilty, destroying the prisoner's hope against hope. The fact that a person is in front of Believers means they are, by definition, culpable. Even the Believers overseeing the space courts are fearful of one another, each one trying to trip another to get ahead. The one greatest lie is the word Democracy. In this reality, Humanity's true nature is to filter out the weak, and, when the population of individuals is small, the brutal pack leaders start to emerge. These leaders are those who can strike fear into the hearts of others with the idea of punishment. This pecking order extends from the absolute pinnacle of the hierarchical dictatorship, the High Priests of the Believers.

The gaps between the stars were bridged long ago: humans have stretched out across the universe. Something about human nature has gnawed its way to the surface: something old and basic in our code. This something screams outwards from our inner being, pulsating deep in our chests, telling us from within that we are doomed to make the same mistakes again and again, powerless to stop the process — helpless in the face of the shadow self of mankind.

Upon descending, we all pull each other downwards, biting and howling — the unsatisfied demons in the deep dark.

To change the nature of humanity there must be a message spread through humanity's rank and file — expanding like a tinder fire, burning hearts and minds — to light a path into the future. A future filled with hope.

CHAPTER THREE

The Letter

Freedom is something that dies unless It's used.

- Hunter . S. Thompson -

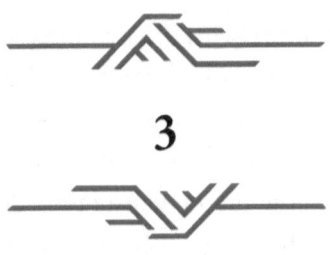

3

David Salem is the prison island's 1,289th Head Guardian. He has a wife, Mary, and his only son is called Tommy. David descends from a very distinguished and vital line of Head Guardians, and he can see no reason why Tommy shouldn't follow suit and become 1,290th Head Guardian on Prison Planet Earth.

Tommy feels that his life within the Drumcroon facility is a monotonous existence that will extend for the rest of his days — a tomb for his thought, a graveyard for his ostentatious ideas and ambitious designs. He cannot help feeling envious of the prisoners' freedom. He feels the cold marble and steel compound killing his mind, dulling his senses. Tommy longs for adventure, far away from the regimented and predictable routine of the facility. He imagines a place in the wild open landscape of his ancestors, on the other side of the island. A place to think, free from the static-like noise that invades his mind, turning all pure and smooth unimpeded thought into grey blocks of nothing — always stacked, always walling him inside.

His only pleasure is his mind; he sculpts and enhances it via the NanoTech Biocovered (NTB) learning pods in the east wing of the compound. The NanoTech Biocovering is living integrated circuitry which can directly interact with a user's brain. His favourite way of relaxing is to climb inside an NTB learning pod and let it bombard him with images from his favourite periods in art — which varies depending on his moods — but never really dated past the 21st century AD (AD here does not stand for the pre-meteorite term Anno Domini, but the post-meteorite term After Dagon. *Dagon* was the alias given to the extinction-level meteorite that nearly ended Homo sapiens — named for an old Mesopotamian god sometimes linked with agriculture, and, importantly, in this case, ploughing). Tommy listens to music; the contemporary music of his day only because all music from the past has been erased in error. No one knows exactly how it happened, but legend has it that in 2039 AD (*Anno Domini*) — when most literature, artwork, and music was located online (or on digital devices) — music became lost, or just stopped working. No explanation was found. Some thought it was the result of a botched computer hacking mission; some attributed it to solar flares. Following the fall of music, records and record players became the most sought-after antiques. They, for whatever reason, had stood the test of time better than any other music storage device. Tommy, having a humble upbringing, has never been able to afford one of these *records*, but he thinks about them often. *How great they must be.*

When he looks at the prisoners, he feels jealous; what these people have, he never could. His father used to say how dangerous these people are. These lunatic prisoners, with their unpredictable, irrational, and lewd behaviour, were the reason the compound he had been born into — and had lived in for sixteen years — had been fortified. There is no doubt that Tommy is extremely safe within the blast walls — guarded by destructive weapons mounted in guard towers, some of which he had helped invent. He had also helped to design the shuttle transport for the prisoners, employing a more sophisticated docking procedure which provides the prisoners a more comfortable end to their journey. It was proving to be efficient, with minimal stress for all involved.

Tommy watches the shuttles come and go, looking on as prisoners cuddle their loved ones. He feels an emotion more powerful than jealousy towards the new prisoners. He sees them as the ones who have stolen his freedom. Without them, he would not be here.

Tommy harbours an intensely deep anger that denies his fellow Guardians' belief system. In Tommy's opinion, the punishment for their crime is the freedom to start again — and yet they cry!

Tommy compares the prisoners' new lives of survival, hunting, and building a home to his own experience of discipline and rules set out by the Guardians. Something extremely basic stirs inside him, some wild part of his nature that screams for adventure.

Months fly past while Tommy prepares his escape. Regulations, and USA dogma make Tommy feel trapped. He gathers clothes, stolen from prisoner transport shuttles, and stores enough food and water for the journey to the nearest prisoner encampment. He imagines how strange it would be to mingle amongst the masses of prisoners in person, as one of them — such an alien experience! — as opposed to seeing only the flashing, coloured lights on the prison map in the Drumcroon facility's control room.

The only way he knows which direction he must travel and how far, as well as the number of prisoners at the nearest community, is from this map. The digital global map in the compound shows extant population figures which are monitored via an implant that prisoners receive upon arrival on Earth. A massive 3D hologram projects the prison planet in a remarkably complex format in the control room, the nucleus of the Drumcroon fortified compound. Tommy finds the hologram fascinating, a thing of immense beauty: the contours of the planet in curving red, dotted colours showing prisoner positions. The danger level of each prisoner is colour coordinated: white for the prisoners considered to be the very worst, followed by yellow, with the prisoners of the least risk in green. The huge control room is where his father spends most of his time. It is his domain, his life, the nexus of control.

The imagined darkness of the lanes and the unknown and exciting future ahead make the night of Tommy's escape the greatest night of his short and uneventful life. His longing to be away from everything he knows is all-consuming. The planning of the escape has been meticulously thought out for some time now — ever since the events of last year.

A heavily pregnant transport prisoner was shot and killed by his father's guards as she tried to escape on a shuttle. It had made no real sense to him. Why had they treated the woman so viciously? Why had the unborn not been allowed to live to grow to the age Tommy is now? To make mistakes of his (or her) own? Tommy's father had tried to counsel him, but his words were cold and in the form of a long and emotionless speech.

'For the greater good' is a commonly bastardised utilitarian term that Tommy has come across many times in the NTB pod, whilst researching different periods throughout history. He has observed that it is often uttered before or after a war, or debauched deeds, to justify cruel actions. Tommy sees 'For the greater good' as the most misused, and traitorously misunderstood, term in history. These four words deluded people; they have been the epithet (the epitaph!) of many evil acts for countless generations — a phrase historically known to start millions of mothers crying for their dead children.

When those four words — 'For the greater good' — fell from his father's lips, Tommy's reservations of leaving evaporated then and there. This was going to be the last time Tommy speaks to his father (aside from the nightly 'goodnight and God bless'), he sneaks away as his parents sleep.

Tommy steals the piece of equipment he is currently working on, what was to be his final commission from the USA. This is his final 'Fuck you!' to the Association. He had been appointed sometime in the spring of last year, by the USA, to find 'new and inventive pathways' in the field of storage and sustainability of energy. Tommy knew what they were saying. They wanted solutions. They wanted advancements. They wanted infinite power. They want... They want...

Tommy had his own agenda. He had used their facilities and their technology and created what he needed to create.

Looking at this small cube as it shimmers violet energy in his palm, he changes his mind. He takes it and he buries it outside of the Facility, near a place where he had played when he was a child. He has no real idea why he does this. Maybe the idea is to retrieve it on his way to the best settlement on the island. Maybe he is just tired of creating the greatest things and then passing them to people who have no real idea of their full potential. Maybe he took and buried the most powerful device ever invented because he did not want whole colonies, on nearby moons and asteroids, destroyed by this device, militarised by power-hungry men and women who condone 'For the greater good.'

This was the only time Tommy Salem did something without planning it, and, like a lot of unplanned things, it did not go well. He was caught trying to escape the facility.

Tommy's great adventure into the unknown has been stolen from him. Stolen, like the prisoners had stolen his life. The effect of his failure to escape was... Crippling.

His memories of that time in his life were patchy: vague shadows, snapshots in black and white. Painful and fast, the sting of a wasp. His mother and father are in the courtroom, they look upset, broken. He tries not to look over to his family, he does not want to know that shame — he realised his father's reputation would now be in tatters.

Tommy's grand escape plan leads to his banishment. Tommy wanted to escape; to leave the compound on his own terms. Instead, he is ordered to leave. Torrents of shame and ridicule, tear-blurred snapshots of hate-filled faces.

His banishment is completed within two days.

Down a concrete tunnel, the heavy metal doors of the compound open automatically. Framed by the grey walls: a hellish storm. A wall of rain jumps inches off the concrete ramp. Bitterly cold air, lightning traces across the dark green and grey sky. The movements of the trees all around the compound is a faint reminder of something beyond the misery of the storm.

Tommy closes his eyes for a second...

"Tell my parents, I'm sorry," says Tommy before walking out into the storm.

As the doors of the compound close, he slumps down on the concrete runway and clutches his cold, hairless head, rocking gently. He sheds a tear or two, but these are washed away by the rain almost as fast as they form. He tries to process a life without his family, he tries to imagine never seeing his mother again.

She's innocent in all this, thinks Tommy. *Just another Optimal person doing Optimal things. Naïve, but innocent and kind.*

He punches himself hard in the jaw, gives his head a wobble, and slings the survival pack onto his back. He grits his now bloodied teeth and screams into the eye of the storm, *"FUCK IT!"*

Tommy sets off in a quick military march. Marching until the wild beat in his chest becomes steady, and his thighs start to feel as though hot needles are slowly being pushed into the muscles. There is the coppery taste of blood in his mouth, his eyes are wild.

The Believers' court issues a 'survival backpack' to all convicts which contains food pouches, water and a first aid kit. This token gesture fulfils their duty of care and should allow the prisoners to survive long enough to reach the closest prisoner community.

It's not right, thinks Tommy. *Nothing about throwing prisoners on an island and leaving them defenceless, exposed to the elements — to fend for themselves against other prisoners, bears, wolves and who knows what else — is right. No, there is no humanity in abandonment — only pain and suffering. Only pain, suffering and this impending sense of... doom.*

SPLINTER SALEM PART ONE

This is all just a bad dream, Tommy thinks. A part of him wants to go back and bang on those large, metal doors and beg for forgiveness, for another chance. A silent, slurring voice in his head — maybe of an ancestor or a malevolent spirit — wants him to head back, scale the wall, and hack off those blaster cannons he had installed just three years ago.

Fuck it all! Thinks Tommy, suddenly furious, *I'll not hack them off! Shit, no! I'll turn my MCL5000-Repeater Cannons on the Guardians and Believers! And — as their heads explode, their arms and legs detach, as volley after volley rip through their chests, tearing out hearts — then they'll see just how much pain they've caused me. And I'll be like, 'Too late, fuckers!'*

Tommy stews with this thought for a long while. It would be so easy for him to do. As he puts distance between himself and the facility, the sinister voice laughing in his head grows ever fainter. He can feel his head starting to heat up. He knows it is only a matter of time now before something bad happens. It always does when this feeling sets in. Whenever an evil idea takes root in Tommy's brain, something ancient and buried deep inside him, a marauding daemon of sorts, turns to face him, lifts a heavy eyebrow and smiles.

Tommy tries to compartmentalise all his hurt and shame, he tries to lock it all away, but it condenses and manifests as a burning lump of hatred in his chest, a pain in his head, and a lump in his throat. All thoughts of his old life are pushed far away by the fierce storm that rages all around him, and within him. An awareness of his surroundings grows. *There's no time*, a dull voice whispers from somewhere deep inside Tommy's mind. He knows his survival depends on reaching his hidden tools. As the concrete fortress disappears in the distance, and the trail of old marble and granite paving stones slowly transform to hard, wet clay, dense undergrowth start to soften the rough clunking of his blast boots.

A thought inside his mind shakes Tommy. Sitting some place where asshole thoughts sit — never in the back of a person's mind, no! — just someplace close enough to unexpectedly sucker-punch him, making Tommy's arms and legs heavy. Five words streak through his heart and mind, like a volley of one of his MCL5000 Cannons.

I have no one now.

A desperate urge to apologise to his mother and father takes hold of him. He feels so many conflicting emotions, but the survival instinct creeps in, like some unwanted, insipid advice from a family member at a funeral. The wind makes the rain attack from right to left now, and the staccato impact of the rain on his cold face reawakens the fury inside. Everything is magnified by the storm — everything is far worse when you are cold. And alone.

Desolate and ruined, his heart is a hollowed-out vessel being filled with the violent rage of the storm.

Bravely or foolishly, he does not know, Tommy Salem fights onward through the rain. He is uncertain exactly how long this path of solitude and coldness will stretch. If Tommy had had any foresight to know the darkness that lay ahead, it would have been a kindness for him to simply sit down and open a vein. To wait for bears to track down the scent and rip him apart.

Tommy hikes for five miles, laboriously, and with heavy feet, through the worse weather prison planet Earth has seen in over one hundred years. A part of him believes he deserves the brutality of the storm, so he soaks up the energy and the pain. Unbeknownst to Tommy, many on this path just curl up and die. Just below the green grass of the island, on either side of him, are many skeletons of those who could not continue. Those who would not, and could not, live. Lying there, buried from sight, the weak of heart and mind, the hopeless, the forgotten.

Tommy feels the sting of something ancient within his being, something inside him turns towards his dim comprehension and smiles. An insane person hiding just out of view. Something more than him. A higher power that soaks into him through his pores, through the many microscopic mouths on his flesh, filling him with something demented, something alien. A channelling of forces — the beginning of a brutal transformation.

That ugly emotion: Revenge. A fearsome look flashes in his eyes, and he imagines what he will do to the high priest of the Believers' court when he eventually meets him. He thinks he will take away his jaw first. Just to watch his tongue loll down as he lets out his last noise.

Tommy kicks a large stone that he imagines to be a priest's shinbone. The rock shoots off and it disturbs a toad, which jumps away, irritated. He stares at the creature for a while, after it stops hopping. The toad seems to wink at Tommy. He wonders how content the little toad must be in the storm.

"At least someone's happy you stupid creature," he mumbles as he strolls away, kicking at a nearby puddle.

The toad jumps up onto a large rock and watches as Tommy enters the woods. The toad never goes into the woods. She knows what is in there. *Stupid creature*, thinks the toad.

Approaching his stash of joining tools, a terrible thought sidles into Tommy's already troubled mind. A smoking thought from an unwelcome place.

He stops. What if a prisoner has found them? What if his joining tools and the Eternal Power Clamp (EPC) have been damaged by a freak bolt of lightning?

Now he runs, panic-stricken, the remaining two hundred metres through the rough grassland. His heart is pounding, there is a metallic taste in his mouth again. He flips planks of wood and branches from the top of a rubbish pile, next to an old, upturned boat. Frantically, he pushes at rocks until he finds the joining tools and sees the EPC shining up at him. Relief floods through him as the precious invention is, once more, back in its creator's possession.

Tommy's heart should have slowed with the elation of retrieving the powerful device, but, instead, it speeds up. Rage builds as all the memories of the Association and the facility flash through his mind. He holds the EPC and the violet energy, swimming inside the transparent box, reminds him of the cost that there is in a power of this magnitude.

"My curse," whispers Tommy, as he studies the violet vortex spiralling — condensing — into a pin prick of nothingness inside the clear, and seemingly empty, box. The force of the surrounding storm, barely reduced by the sheltering trees, keeps him on edge. A torrent of memories assails him, inside, as the storm relentlessly pummels the external woods. He sees his father's eyes filled with disappointment. He sees his mother's gaunt, distraught face in the Believers' court. Like so many before him, his liberation was realised through the tears of others.

Tommy presses the indents of the joining rods and points them towards the wreck of the rowboat. A line of neon light shoots out of the end of each rod, followed by a blast of fire. The flame is like the breath of the mythical dragon. It leaps forth, searching out, licking the damp carcass of the old, upturned boat. Fascinated, he watches the blues and greens of the flames as they peel away layers of the old ship's paint, the boat revealing its true self to the flame. The flame heats his flesh and warms his soul. He sighs with relief that the machinery — which he has invested so much time designing — still has life. In the rain, the boat continues to crackle and hiss in the face of the raw elemental, and opposite, energy of fire and water combined. Tommy finds a strange amusement in the raw power that he has unleashed.

The flame seems a mirror to his very wild, and increasingly aggressive, nature. With the boat still burning, hissing in the rain, he presses the long metal joining tools together, placing them on his right arm. The rods attach to bio-ports on his arm and stick out inches over the back of his clenched fist. He places the cube-shaped EPC underneath the joining rods on his forearm. Vibrations start. Vein-like implants begin to snake around under Tommy's flesh. He takes a sharp intake of air through pursed lips. This part always hurts him, but it can not be done any other way. The ability to suffer massive levels of pain is, he modestly believes, a recognisable part of his genius. It has always been a factor in his complicated and unfortunate life. He has always taken pain and recognised it as a lesson. He accepts that an unwanted beating is sometimes necessary to keep the peace, knowing all the time that he is strong enough to endure more. Always.

The balance of pain to pleasure is a law not yet understood. Tommy's informed guess would be that good things might just balance the bad in his life, if he searched hard for them.

Power surges through his veins, as the vines of liquid information light up complex networks, changing muscle to something more. The technological abominations of a very unusual child's imagination join, painfully, with hard, material reality.

Tommy knows the worst pain is to come, as his mechanical arm prepares for the next stage. He braces himself as he runs his left hand over the Eternal Power Clamp, glowing violet and pulsating slightly on his right forearm. A tendril of violet matter sits in his hand, turning red and fizzing in the rain. It shape-shifts, becoming an oval. Tommy gulps in two deep breaths and slaps it into his left eye socket. He grinds his teeth as it melts into his eyeball and bone, bonding with him, completing the MechVision.

Dampened pastel colours are visible under his skin, swirling in patches then vanishing. The twisting colours are seen on his forehead, then disappear only to reappear further down his arm, then under his eye. The pain subsides to a low drum beat as the evolution of this bio-bonding nears completion. The final — much less painful — stage is another quick swipe of the EPC, now glowing a violet colour just beneath the surface of his arm. A violet liquid energy moves and soaks into his left palm. He stares a while. It fascinates Tommy to see the EPC's purple energy creating a whirlpool inside his hand.

He imagines small ships carrying people round and round, down and down, towards the pinprick centre of that violet vortex in his hand — spiralling down until they vanished inside that beautiful display of Power Clamp energy.

Readings appear in his left eye's MechVision, assessing and analysing properties, making subtle, pre-programmed alterations for this expensive equipment to work to its maximum capability.

Diagnostics complete, Tommy stomps off in his large, metal blast boots. He strides onwards through the driving rain, into the dense woodland area behind the carcass of the still-burning boat. His EPC-infused arm shimmers like the scales of a wet fish.

The boat fire can still be seen from far away, continuing to emit sounds of fierce disapproval as the moisture in the wood is chased out by the changing yellow, blue and green flames. Tommy's frustration and anger have driven him deep into the woods. His MechVision scouts the tall, evergreen trees for the perfect branches to use to build a shelter. Locating some branches, his CerebroTech calculates the vertical impact needed at an elevation of 36.75 ft. He hovers, and circles, his glowing left hand over the length of the rods jutting out from his right arm. The violet colour of his left-hand winks, dimmer then brighter.

"Grappling hooks: tree climb," Tommy says, as the two rods vibrate under the glow. A split second of energy surges through his altered right arm, shooting from fist to shoulder, as the two rods change shape into a set of barbed grappling hooks. Like he is trying to rid his boot of mud, he backheels his left blast boot into a stone that is trapped in the anaconda-like roots of an ancient evergreen. Nothing happens. Another, this time more substantial, backward hoof and success comes in the form of a curved, serrated blade, one inch thick, which springs out from the circumference of the boot.

"Dumb blades," he mutters.

Tommy repeats the process for the right foot and, to his relief, this blade springs out at the first tap of his heel. He backs away from the giant tree and stares upwards. He lifts his arm until it aligns with his MechVision identified target position.

"Bam!" Tommy shouts, as the curved, silver hooks launch, towing behind them, with a zipping noise, a golden cable from the joining rods.

Upon hearing the sharp sound of impact, Tommy mentally commands the wire to reel him up. He bangs into the side of an adjacent tree.

"Ah, damn!" yells Tommy.

Tommy's CerebroTech struggles to comprehend his latest 'instruction', which results in him being reeled faster and faster through the mass of branches. Tommy's cursing intensifies, prompting further acceleration. Before he knows it, he is part of a vicious circle of shouting and swearing and being smashed in the face by bits of trees, at high speed. This short, sharp trip leaves him with nasty scratches to his left cheek and brow. His empty stomach churns, his fragile mental state tips closer to a complete breakdown.

With the first large bow of the tree level with Tommy, he digs the serrated-blade boots into the trunk of the tree and tests the weight. He frees his left hand and waves violet light over the grapple hooks and thinks of a cutting device. Within seconds the grappling hooks shape-shift into a spinning disc cutter with angry looking violet teeth. He puts the fearsome device into effect and revels in the smell as his spinning disk melts through the pine tree branch, separating it from the main trunk with ease. The scent of pine fills Tommy with a burst of joy and a feeling of belonging he cannot explain. He waits and stares at the branch. It is severed, but not moving. This never happened whilst attending training exercises in the NTB training rooms at the facility! Tommy sees the branch is resting on other, lower branches. Tommy's left eye glows slightly as his brain asks another problem to be solved. Tommy stares at the branch, then at the woodland floor that is so far below him. Satisfied with the CerebroTech calculations, he changes his arm from cutting disc back to the grappling hooks, then attaches them to the large branch before leaping from the tree. His weight dislodges the branch slowly as the golden cable pays out, slowing his descent as the floor of the forest approaches. He hits the ground and rolls away from the falling wood.

The mighty branch crashes down a few feet behind him. The CerebroTech may have worked out the distance and mass of the branch, but the idea and timing of the manoeuvre is all Tommy.

Tommy had kept himself busy during the long days in the facility, but nights were the worst time. Nights of crippling solitude. Nights where his intelligence became a drunk and abusive jailer. The despair and finality of his pre-planned life stretched out before him. Pointlessness stabbed at his heart. The longing to be something other than a trapped human, with all the fleshy weaknesses that came with the role, played like a faulty recording over and over, until the noise became deafening. He wishes he is something better, something stronger — a machine whose cogs never rust.

To be denied his quiet getaway. To get caught, mid-escape, by the stupid, lesser beings: Guardians. Tommy felt robbed of victory.

And now here is dragging this branch through the wet woods, freedom achieved. But at what cost? He curses under his breath as he struggles with the awkward limb of the evergreen. The only calming presence is the smell of the freshly chopped pine. He breathes in the aroma and sighs. The smell is like nothing he has experienced. The sap coats his pale hands, the smell joined to his skin like the EPC to his arm. Unlike his device, the calming smell would disappear with time.

Tommy arrives back at the boat fire in the hinterland of the wood. The now settled-in fire is emitting just the right amount of heat, the roaring flames long since gone. The occasional flash of yellow spins up, now and again, within the deeper hues of the glowing orange and the red veins burning in the wood. The boat still hisses as the ancient elements of water and fire wage their eternal battle.

Here, the battle is one-sided. Tommy knows this is the case, as the joining rods had coated the wood with a flammable substance; something that the cylinders generate inside them to keep them fresh when they are dormant and unused. Water battles on, without full knowledge of Fire's secret advantage, as glowing orange plasma makes disorganised, jagged grids on the dark shadow of the hull. Fizzing and crackling with ancient purpose, the fire consumes more of the ship. Tommy makes a makeshift shelter at the edge of the clearing, gathering more wood from sheltered areas. *There are plenty of places worth searching*, Tommy thinks — trying hard to stay positive.

Hunger gnaws Tommy's stomach like a gastric ulcer as he climbs into his shelter and tests the layers of springy pine branch flooring — its purpose is to keep his body from the wet floor, and to allow the heat from the fire to circulate beneath him. He spreads out a survival blanket, which unfolds from a small side pouch in the survival bag given to him by the Believers' court.

He unlatches the provisions bag, looking for pouches of food. Tommy finds a water flask first and he drinks deeply. Being dehydrated, the water feels like it does not reach his stomach. It feels as if the water is being absorbed through his oesophagus, stealing the liquid before it can reach his walnut-sized stomach. He sighs heavily, rubs his forehead, and gives in to the tiredness, sinking into the springy pine mattress. His pale hands shake, clasped over his face, as the rainwater drips into his shelter.

Tommy takes time to concentrate on his breathing, calming his heart. He searches the main compartment of the silver-grey, bland-coloured rucksack for further provisions. It surprises him to find his mother's home-made bread and he opens a ceramic pot of his mother's strawberry jam. Ripping up clumps of bread, he scoops up the godly preserve and gobbles it down. Sweetness and tartness galvanise his saliva glands into action, making his eyes water and his face scrunch up with pleasure. He rifles through the other supplies in a quick inventory, as rain continues to pelt down all around. Lightning bolts flash somewhere behind him. He turns, not sure why he does, and counts, just like his mother taught him when he was a toddler. One ...Two ...Thr — a thunderclap explodes, seeming to rock the very trees. So, the storm is about three kilometres away. Physics that even a small child can manage, even if they do not understand the maths.

Tommy continues his stocktake and finds a small silver packet of food, which is awful, but has in it all the things the body requires. A medical bag is attached to the outside of the pack, the symbol of the USA on the front, glimmering in the light. He scowls at it, cursing under his breath, swearing to never use *their* things to heal himself — even if his arm is hanging off. He unzips the pack to look at what is in there. There is a jar of unguent to treat minor scrapes. He pops the top off it and pettily empties it on to the floor, throwing the jar away for good measure. As he moves aside various bandages, tucked away, under various other medical survival equipment, he finds a letter clearly written in his mother's scrupulous hand.

Tommy stares, swallowing hard and choking back a sob, as he firmly zips the letter back into the bag. He gulps down the last of the water from his flask, then he lodges it in the roof of the shelter to capture some more water for his long journey to the other side of the Island. He sucks at his fingers, rubbing the remnants of the sticky jam away on the legs of his cadet uniform pants. Grimacing, he paints the troubled look of a person many years his senior onto his face, eyes transfixed on the bag. He imagines what horrors lie in wait in those Goddamned words.

Tommy points the joining rods towards the fire, from the opening of his den, and releases another fireball into the boat campfire. He darts out into the rain and throws several large logs on the fire, with accompanying hissing, as if the flames get have an opinion on this.

"I'm reading it! Fuck it! I don't care!" Tommy says to the stoic, non-judgmental flames. He springs back into the den and feverously fishes out his mother's letter. Drenched now from the bitter storm, but not cold, Tommy reads the letter, and his head begins to pound and heat up. The embarrassment and shame he felt in the court overwhelms him once more. He remembers again, with heart-rending detail, his mother crying in court. She is the one person in this world who has his back, the one person who he trusts — and she is heartbroken by his actions.

Still reading, his shame is soon turned to self-pity, as Mary Salem proclaims her unconditional love for Tommy, but that she does not know how to deal with the loss of her son, her only child. He pauses, his heart screaming for his mother's pain. Her loss. His loss!

During this pause he notices that there is writing on the other side. Thinking it might be more from his mum, he flips the page over, but the hand there is clearly the severe, angled copperplate of his father. As he reads, he notes the tone is altogether dissimilar to that used by his mother. His father writes in a dismissive, emotionless, tone. Practical to the point of inanity, insulting his son's prodigious intellect. There were warnings of the dangers of the forest and, beyond that, the Lanes, and the surrounding areas of the coast. After that, the letter becomes an attack on his behaviour. His father said Tommy's vast intelligence and creative genius in many fields of invention, which had opened doors to golden opportunities, were sabotaged by his 'unpredictable, destructive tendencies combined with unfathomable hubris.' Instead of love, his father was telling him things he already knew and committing an assassination of his character.

The EPC starts to make a *Vrrrrrr* noise. Tommy clasps the letter harder than he has squeezed anything before. He squeezes until his knuckles crack and whiten. He grasps it as if the words might fuse with his flesh, like the liquid integrated circuits that are coursing through him, but the words remain inert and alien. He crushes the letter, as if somehow this would change his father's harsh words into something better — but ... no. This message is the final push. Despite all of

Tommy's intellect and subtlety of mind, the last word is always with the father. The final tipping of Tommy's ill-balanced mental state, the final judgement of his character, he lets his anger better his sense as he springs out of his den. He moves as if in a dream.

"Hubris?" he shouts at the nearest tree, as he projects his hurt emotions upon a wooden version of his father. CerebroTech stymied by this non-command, his arm shudders in confusion of what is being asked.

"I'll show you fucking *hubris*!" A ball of violet energy blasts out, and the tree explodes.

He rubs at his throbbing head with his left hand. His eyes clamp shut as the rain bombards his upturned face. The storm cooling his mood for a little while, he tries to calm himself. But the words keep coming. Words of hurt come spewing into his head, from his father, words of mourning, seemingly unending, pour into his mind from his mother's broken heart. These words are a tempest in Tommy's head — a maelstrom of the mind — and they cause his mental well-being to topple into the furnace flames at the core of him. There, a fiery face looks deep into his soul, reading those painful, burning words ... and *smiles*.

CHAPTER FOUR
Demon in a Cave

Generosity is giving more than you can, and pride is taking less than you need.

-Khalil Gibran-

4

Tommy's primal scream is so loud it feels like a bomb going off in his head. His MechVision, acting on his unspoken, mental commands, chooses a target — an arborary representation of his father. Glowing violet orbs of raw energy streak from his arm and reduce the tree to flying shards. Another target is selected and instantly destroyed, consumed in a flash of raw, uncontrollable, violet lightning: the mighty power of his Eternal Power Clamp.

Trees fragment in all directions. Some embed themselves in Tommy, but he is numb. His fierce rage keeps him standing despite the mounting injuries he is sustaining. Peppered by pieces of tree, he turns in a semi-circle, spreading oblivion in his wake, rain lashing across his face. Tasting his own blood but unable — unwilling — to stop, Tommy spins, screaming and firing. Trees die. Animals and insects sheltering in the trees are vaporised. His elemental fury is the channelled despair of the memory of every night he had spent in the facility's shadow: carrying out their commands, witnessing their atrocities. All this hate

— this division — flows through his conflicted self to the contrapuntally-named 'joining tool' on his arm.

He levels everything in sight, at the centre of an expanding sphere of destructive violet light, and this chaos unfurls to the sound of laughter.

An ancient and evil laugh, welling from deep within him.

Tommy never feels the blow to the back of his head. There is a hollow noise of impact and a strong vibration that shakes his eyeballs in their sockets and expels the air from his lungs. Then there is just the welcome embrace of darkness. Release from thought, from feeling —from pain. Then ...

...dragging...

...weightlessness...

...blurred images of trees passing at high speed.

Warm blood is coursing from his skull, stinging his eyes. His battered body aches with the pain of a thousand shrapnel wounds as the adrenaline leaves his bloodstream.

His breathing slows and he is in a state of confusion — clearly concussed and in shock. He is only vaguely aware of his jerky movement through the forest canopy.

Tommy is being thrown over branches and caught as if his weight is nothing! Being upside down, slumped over the right shoulder of the speedy fiend who assaulted him, the blood flows down to — and out of! — his head. His head pounding, Tommy alternates between consciousness and the dark place that no one escapes from for long.

Sometimes he hears his heart thumping away in his temples, rhythmically pumping away his lifeblood from his head wounds. Sometimes, somehow, he hears the powerful and steady beat of his captor's alien heart through his hard, scaly back. *Scaly?* Maybe he was hallucinating?

Blood loss, and the building pressure in Tommy's skull, becomes too much for him. Darkness creeps in on him once more, and this time he does not wake for a long time.

———— ╫╫╲╲╁╫╫ ————

Tommy's consciousness edged towards him as timorously as a mouse. Senses recognised things piecemeal, as if putting together a particularly difficult jigsaw puzzle. The soothing pulse of waves on rock. The harsh shrieks of distant seagulls. The strong iodine tang of seaweed in his nostrils.

He struggles to open both eyes. Only one of his eyes obeys, revealing the warring collage of dark, green grey, flecked with white, of the storm-tossed sea as it smashes on the rocks far below him. It is jerkily getting nearer. He is in a makeshift sling, slick with rain, and is slowly being winched down a cliff face. Struck with confusion and fear, he tries to look round to see the person responsible. Halfway down the cliff faces, a powerful man swings him outwards, toward the sea. Too weak to scream, Tommy lets out a startled whimper as the sling that is carrying him streaks out and then, suddenly, turns and heads back, pendulum-like. Arms and legs bound, he knows that he is going to be smashed head-first into the cliff-face, but he cannot prevent it.

Tommy braces himself as he sees the cold, unfeeling wall of the cliff approaching at speed, and then ... warmth. No impact. No bone-grinding collision. No more rain. Only gentle hands holding him. Shadows dance in the cave's firelight and Tommy notices bustling figures speaking in a foreign tongue. He flails, helplessly. Too weak. Fading fast. His brain hazily notes an unwanted damage report from his MechVision, and he sinks once more into the painless oblivion of unconsciousness.

For days he seesaws back and forth in consciousness, like a witch on a ducking stool. Fragments of memory. Thoughts too hard to organise. Many missing items. On the fourth day, Tommy opens his eyes and thankfully finds he can keep them open. But he cannot move. He finds himself upright, bound in a cross shape with both arms and legs outstretched. A cold object is placed delicately to Tommy's throat and he feels a sharp tugging at his skin. Is someone stitching his neck? His eyes take in the dimly lit cave.

"You're from the facility, yes?" a low, gravel-filled voice says in Tommy's right ear. Not really a question. His head flinches away from the warm, stale-smelling breath. It smells of clay, of blood and sulphur.

Tommy's joining tool whirs and charges with power as his panic and fear convinces him to fight.

"Ah, ah, ah," says the voice, as a cold, sharp blade threatens to open his throat.

"W-, wh-, what, d-, d-, do you, w-, want with me!" Tommy says, shaking with dread.

For a while there is silence.

Somehow, he can sense the eyes of his fiend-like captor watching him. He imagines the creature smirking in the dark, contemplating which part of Tommy he will eat first. Tommy's futility burst forth as rage.

"Untie me, you bastard! I'll blast you to pieces!" Tommy's arm glows and the rods begin to fizz with violet energy.

The blade at Tommy's throat loosens. "Listen to me!" the voice booms. "I will let you fly. I will. I will let you go. But you have to promise me that you will not use this ...*contraption* —" here the blade was moved from his throat to tap on his metal arm "— around my family." Even in the low light of the cave, Tommy sees the knife, tapping on the joining tools of his right arm. The edge looks over ten inches. It is dark, curved, razor sharp, and the perfect shape for slicing a throat. Tommy blinks several times. The sweat on his brow runs into his eyes. Strangely, he feels mild relief that this butchers-tool belongs to a family-oriented person.

"I promise," says Tommy in a steady voice that belied his nerves. "I assure you I will not use it. Why would I hurt you, or your family? I don't even know you."

He pauses, thinking.

"Anyway, *you're* the one who attacked *me*! You knocked me out, and kidnapped me, and brought me to this dark hovel!" The blade instantly comes back to Tommy's throat, the pressure redoubled.

"This *...hovel...*" His captor says carefully, as if the word is distasteful, "is my family's home. It has been this way for hundreds of years. And, furthermore, I *saved* you. I saved you from yourself. I brought you to my home and let my daughter heal your broken body. That saved you from death. So, since you have made your promise to me, I will make one to you. If I feel, at any time, that you — or this device attached to you — is a threat to my family, or my home, I will kill you. This I promise. I will rip you apart. Piece by piece. *Slowly.*"

Tommy does well to supress a shudder. "Okay, okay, I'm sorry," says Tommy. "The arm is a tool. It's not designed to hurt," continues Tommy, moving his altered arm in its leather restraints. The blade falls into view again, swishing close to Tommy's eyes. He involuntarily arches his head back away from the cruel edge. The voice in the dark speaks again.

"And *this* is my tool. It, too, is not intended to hurt. But it can be used to devastating effect. Especially on people who threaten the safety of my clan. I don't want a repeat of the behaviour I saw in the forest; I don't want to have to kill you."

The blade drops from Tommy's vision.

"I understand, I understand. Honestly, I'm not dangerous. I just... I..." Tommy flicks his head from left to right, trying to put a face to the voice in the darkness, trying to see behind him — but to no avail. All he succeeds in doing is making his head throb even more.

"Please, show yourself. Let's talk this through, face to face."

The voice speaks again, but softly this time.

"I shall show myself to you, but I will warn you. I ...do not look ...as others do. Try not to be scared, young Tommy. I am not your enemy."

Tommy is intrigued by the words, but a sudden realisation hits him. "How do you know my name?"

"I read your letter."

"That's private!" Tommy snaps, seeming to forget his precarious position.

"It's a wonderful letter. It's possibly what saved your life. That ... and your arm. Although, I must admit, I had thought about chopping it off. Then again, I'm no monster..."

Tommy's mysterious captor steps into view and Tommy's eyes widen in horror.

Standing in front of him was a horned demon.

"What the *Hell* are you?"

"I'm not sure how to take those words. Particularly, coming from a kid who's covered in wood and glowing stuff," The being — the man? — smiles. Instead of teeth, the grin reveals a serrated sheet of bone, broken in places.

"My name is Talon."

Talon moves backwards and more of this apparition is visible to Tommy.

Great, Tommy thinks, *a loincloth-wearing freak-of-nature...*

"It's dark in here for a reason, young Tommy. My appearance in full light can ..." Whilst talking, the individual known as Talon takes a moment to light a pre-made fire in the centre of the cavern. Smoke swirls up through a tunnel-vent in the roof. Tommy does not see Talon move, but his voice seems to come from the left of him, and then from the right, as he lights two wall torches, and then the devil appears again right in front of him. As the light in the cave brightens, Talon finishes his sentence, "...instil a strange feeling of disgust in people of a weaker disposition. This is an understandable reaction."

With the greater illumination, the features of Talon's skin are revealed. Bedazzling and frightening at the same time. Mystical runes cover the entirety of his dark, leather-like skin. His horned face is a thing from nightmares. Still smiling his serrated smile, his cavernous eyes seem to study Tommy's glowing arm.

Tommy stares at Talon's body and notices further terrifying features. On his arms, bony structures protrude out of his flesh at each of his elbows, forming lethal-looking scimitars over a foot in length. Talon's knees are formed into curved hook-like horns, five-inch-wide at the base. His knee-horns seem to compliment, at least in shape, the two thinner, shorter horns at his temple. His cheekbones also have clusters of spikes that protrude through his skin, like weaponised warts. The larger spikes are in the centre of his cheek and these get smaller and smaller, leading to barnacle-size carbuncles at the outermost edges of Talon's face. His powerful jaw and heavily spiked chin form a most violent beard.

At the end of Talon's arms Tommy receives another shock.

"Those are your fingers!" says Tommy, as he realises what was held to his throat seconds ago. Talon's hands end in long, bone-bladed, ebony fingers.

He quietly appraises the deadly blades of the grinning monster.

"You're sure you're not going to kill me, aren't you?" Tommy says, nervously. *Afterall, what else do horned monsters from nightmares do aside from killing and eating people?*

"You'd taste bad with all that ...stuff ...inside you. Besides which, I'm all out of garlic," Talon jokes, guessing Tommy's thoughts from the rictus of his face.

"I would have killed you in the woods, had I wanted to, yes?"

Shocked out of a response which would make any sense, Tommy just stares. Things too fast to identify shoot past Tommy, to his outstretched arms, slicing through the ties that bind him to the cross.

"I can see why you're called Talon," Tommy says, as he rubs feeling back into his wrists. He tries to test his legs with a few uneasy and painful steps, but this proves too much for Tommy in his weakened state. Talon helps him over to a rabbit pelt-covered bed, behind the makeshift cross.

"Here, here. Sit, now, or lay down. You need rest. To heal," Talon says lowering him to the comfortable bed.

"What's wrong with me? Everything hurts when I move. Did you do all this damage to me?"

Tommy is now aware of the stitches, one row after another, like caterpillars, causing tightness on his legs, upper arms and across his chest. He touches his face to find stitches over his forehead and left cheek.

"What's happened? Did you do this to me! Are you making me into a monster like you?"

"*RELAX!*" Talon booms back. The volume of Talon's stentorian outburst causes Tommy's ears to ring, and the noise echoes around the cave. It almost seems to silence the tide outside.

As the peal of thunder, Talon's voice, fades, he says more softly, "I knocked you out with a log. That is all, little one."

"That's all?" Tommy says with disdain. He pulls his survival jacket off to see the full extent of his injuries.

"Saturn's moons ... What the fuck is all this?"

"You did it to yourself. When you destroyed many trees with that ...that ...whatever that thing is you have attached to your arm! You're too stupid for such a powerful right arm. You're just a dumb Guardian with a magic arm," Talon says with an odd smirk.

Tommy puts his head in his hands and quietens a scream. Keeping his hands over his face, to hide tears of rage, he tries to wish this sorry predicament away. He hopes this is merely a dream. A nightmare. An illusion. Perhaps, some deep-fake reality of an NTB room he has fallen into, accidentally. Caught in the *Hell Lights*. It was a well-known military phenomenon. Soldiers that could speak afterwards, who had not turn into gibbering wrecks, describe unreal and horrific journeys. Even the toughest of soldiers transform into cowering husks after falling foul of the things that lurk in the Marianas trench of their own psyche.

This must be NTB-generated Hell Lights, thinks Tommy. This is his psychically generated scenario: to eke out the rest of his painful days in a cave with a demon. A demon which may or may not eat him. Maybe the demon represents his inner evil. Or his lust. Or something equally Freudian. No, this cannot be reality. It must be NTB.

When he removes his damaged hands from his scarred face, and wipes his tears away, there is a bowl of hot liquid in front of him.

"Drink it; it will strengthen you. Make sure you finish it, though."

"Thank you," Tommy says, not sure he means it. He examines the liquid, sniffs it a little, but makes no move to drink it. Talon is now crouching across from Tommy, staring into the fire and drinking deeply from a similar wooden bowl. Tommy copies him and feels the liquid burning down his throat and heating his core. It is the first time in so many days that he has felt any comfort. They finish their drink at the same time.

"Good?" inquires Talon, raising horned eyebrows and collecting the bowl. Tommy nods.

"Thank you," Tommy repeats, as his pain subsides enough for him to lie back. Talon shrugs.

"It's Daria who deserves your thanks. My daughter pulled out many splinters from you and stitched your wounds. I'm not very proficient with a needle, you see." Talon flicks his lethal blades out in a fan shape before raising his little finger out towards Tommy.

"She pulled out one as large as this."

Tommy stares at the large, pointed digit, shudders, snuggles deeper into bed, pulling the rabbit pelt coverlet further over himself for warmth.

Tommy tries moving onto his side to get more comfortable, but the smallest of movements cause him excruciating pain.

He studies the walls of the cave for a little while, anything to distract from this harsh reality. He could see Talon pulling back what appeared to be a cavern wall, revealing a shelf for bowls. Clearly some sort of camouflage tech. This camouflage material appears to cover the cavern wall to wall. Tommy remembers the echoes of Talon's voice when Talon yelled at him. This cave must just be one room in an entire system of linked caves. Tommy wants to turn his hypothesis — that of an interlocking cave system — into a reality by getting up and physically exploring. But he just hurts too badly. Maybe the adventuring can wait.

The fire is now in full blaze. Tommy wants to feel warm, but he is clammy and cold. He feels cold sweat running down his head, funnelling down his stitched flesh. The sting of his sweat in newly stitched wounds causes him to feel sick. Talon adds a dried log to the fire, and it seems to crackle with anticipation, reaching up yellow, dancing arms which twine around the wood, climbing higher. Talon grabs another log from behind another camouflaged curtain that is on the ground near Tommy. He places this second log into the flames, an amber embrace spitting forth a myriad of sacred tonal changes. Tommy stares through the flames towards the hidden cave entrance as light from outside suddenly floods the cave. The extra light is soon gone, as the camouflage veil falls back into place, and a small shape darts towards Talon, leaping into his dangerous arms. A toddler nuzzles into Talon's muscular, rune-etched chest.

"My Angel, where have you been?" Talon whispers to this surprisingly normal looking infant, as she squirms to get even closer to her doting father.

"I've just been fishing with Thankwell," says Daria with a contented sigh.

"What did you catch?"

"Lots of things."

"What did Thankwell catch?"

"The same. Where is Astilla, papa? He's not gone, has he? You've not eaten him, have you, Papa?"

Talon shoots a look over to Tommy. "No, I've not eaten him. Not yet, anyway." Talon then winks over towards Tommy as he holds his normal looking infant.

Taking a deep breath of the fresh sea air, which had drifted in with Daria, Tommy asks the obvious question.

"This... is your kin?" Tommy struggles to sit up but the pain stops him.

"Astilla, you're still here! ...And you're awake!" Daria springs out of her father's arms and is next to Tommy in a heartbeat. Talon chuckles as Tommy tries to block the frantic hands of the toddler stroking his head like some sort of new pet.

"She's the one who treated my injuries? She must be — what? — five?"

"No, she's not, you silly goose ... She's three!" corrects the beaming Daria. "I like to fix people; I always treat Papa's boo boos. I'll be a doctor one day."

Tommy's confusion at this precocious child could not be any greater. He stares from Talon's frightening smile to his daughter's beaming smile. Talon pulls Daria away from the injured Tommy as he can see that her constant pawing is causing him some discomfort. Finding it hilarious, he picks her up into his arms and kisses the top of her head as she tries to free herself. She wriggles — her legs kicking fast, faster — and then, suddenly, her legs blur with ferocious speed, buzzing like a fly's wings.

"Aww, Astilla!" Daria laughs as her father blows raspberries on her neck. "Help, help!" she says, giggling.

"Go on now. Leave poor Tommy alone and go and see what Thankwell is doing."

"No...No, Papa, Thankwell's sleeping."

"Oh, the big lazy lump," Talon says, as the neck raspberries continue.

"Ha, ha, get off! Can I show Astilla what I pulled out of him, Papa?"

"I'm sure poor Tommy doesn't wish to be reminded..."

"No...It's okay," Tommy says, shifting with a pained groan into a sitting position. "I want to see them. I *need* to see them."

Daria, clearly seeing his discomfort, springs from her father's arms and darts out of Tommy's sight. Tommy and Talon exchange glances. Returning in an instant, Daria smiles as she drags the covers off her bed to add more support behind Tommy's sore back. She loves having a real patient.

"Thank you, Daria," Tommy says through gritted teeth. The pain of movement is almost unbearable.

Daria smiles, strokes his head and she looks over towards her father. Tilting her angelic little head, fluttering her long eyelashes, she stares a silent question. Talon stares back at her, quizzically at first, then, finally understanding, he raises his hands in assent.

"Okay, okay, okay! You always get your own way, you spoilt little child! Well on with it, then! Your endless pestering is unsettling the poor boy. Hurry it up! And then let Tommy rest!"

"Ok, Papa."

Despite Talon's mock anger and fearsome appearance, at that moment all Tommy sees is a father who is frustrated, yet amused, at being unable to deny the wishes of his beloved child.

Daria scurries away past Tommy, her tiny little surgeon hands rubbing together. She goes towards the back of the cave, where Tommy sees another small bed, presumably where his extra blanket originated. She picks up what looks like an upside-down old metal helmet of some long-lost tribe and returns with such speed it shocks Tommy almost as much as the grinning horror that is Talon.

"Ooh, no, silly me! ... I dropped one."

She blurs a trail to the other bed and back again. It takes seconds. Tommy manages a smile through the pain this time.

"You're a fast one, aren't you, Daria?"

"Look at all these, Astilla." Daria holds out the ancient metal headwear.

"What the ..." Tommy says, under his breath "So... many ... too ...too much."

The Helmet is packed full of blood-soaked shards of wood that range in length from one inch to seven. Sickness and aching surges through Tommy's body now. This toddler in front of him had pulled this shrapnel from his flesh. This child had operated on his body — in this very cave.

"Did I do good, Astilla?" Daria asks, smiling and nodding.

Tommy takes deep, gulping breaths. He tries to regain composure as the blood drains from his face. His ashen face tingles. Daria places the helmet of horror onto the floor next to Tommy and paws at Tommy's stitch-crossed face. She strokes her hand over his ruffled hair several times, like he is her human pet. She tilts her head from side to side, like a confused dog.

"Aww — you, aww," she says lovingly, before pulling out, from where she was hiding it behind her back, a huge wooden stake to show him.

"This is the really big, bad boo boo maker! Grrrrr!

"This can't be real. This is NTB. This can't be real." Tommy throws up and then passes out. As he passes out, he hears the rumbling laughter of Talon and the worried, birdlike voice of Daria repeatedly chirping, "Poor Astilla. Aww. Poor, poor, Astilla."

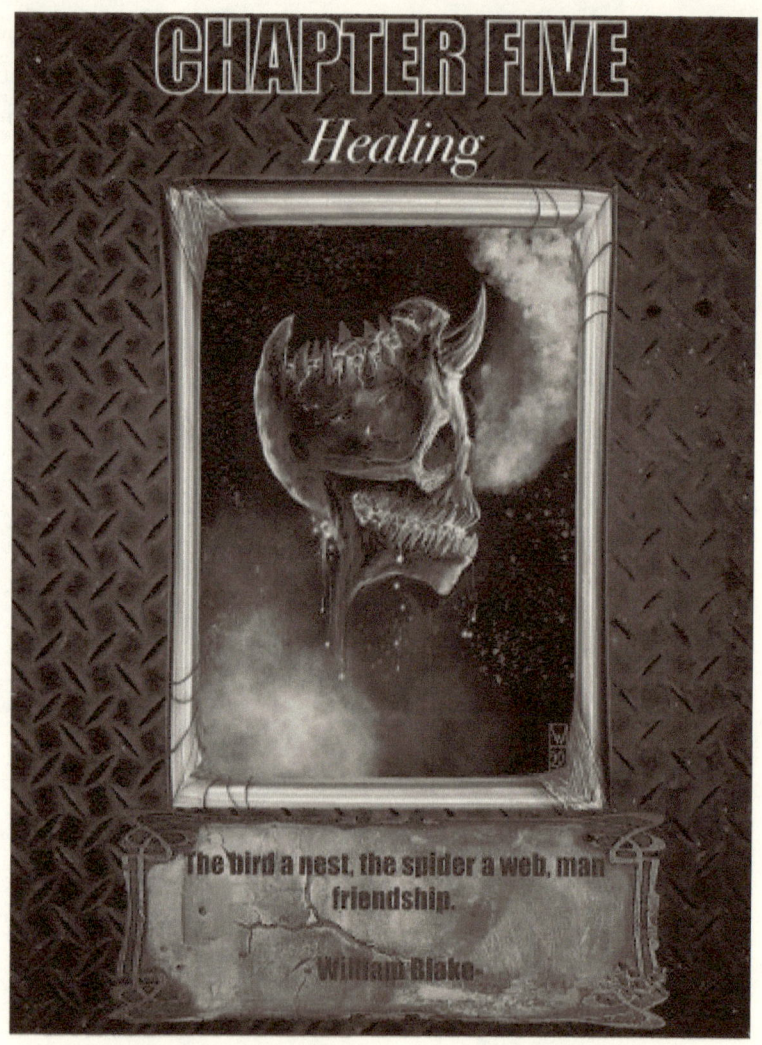

CHAPTER FIVE
Healing

The bird a nest, the spider a web, man friendship.

-William Blake-

5

$\mathbf{A}$ terrible fever consumes Tommy. Daria cradles his head, during the

worst times, singing soft lullabies in a foreign tongue, unidentifiable

and ancient.

Tommy stares upwards at the knot-work rope ceiling. Pain, heat, confusion — and then the ropes come for him. They climb down the cavern walls and wrap around his neck, slither into his nasal cavities — choking him from the inside — filling his lungs and blocking his throat. In the flickering, dim light of the fire, the ropes swirl and dance. And sometimes, just sometimes, the shadow of a horn-faced demon is seen.

Tommy's nightmares continue...

Inside a concrete coffin, the devil is scratching a lullaby on the slab covering the tomb while his parents cry and hold one another at the graveside. They watch him being lowered into the earth. His magical arm blasts through the concrete, and he takes deep breaths of air. *Free!* His arm then turns into a mechanical boa constrictor that coils around his body while Tommy looks to his parents for help, choking for words as well wishers throw flowers on his head. The fever brings another nightmare, even more haunting than being buried alive.

Underground, running at high-speed down an earthy tunnel, the damp clay earth filling his lungs, his heart pounding. He looks at his arms, his hands; his fingers are blades — he is Talon. There are echoes of screaming. Dark laughter rings in his ears. It seems to come from far inside the earth, deep down, as if the earth is alive with noise. As if the noise is the sound of the Earth's beating heart. His senses are heightened, his vision is altered. The twisting tunnel of dirt, the spiral roots and the boulders are all illuminated by some supernatural inner ability to see at night. There are no torches on the walls, no light this far down under the ground, and yet he can see the very finest details. The tunnel opens out into a massive cavern. The chill of the air in the vast palatial chamber is refreshing after the long journey down the narrow, claustrophobic tunnel. Stalactites hang from the roof like dark chandeliers. Stalagmites reaching up to meet some of them, forming fragile pillars.

The underground kingdom — for that is what it is — greets him with such grand sights. It is littered with carved busts of strange creatures from an unidentifiable race, old swords, guns, piles of jewels, crowns and shields, interspersed with demonic masks made of metal, clay and wood. These all lead to the centre of the underground cathedral where a huge circular stone stage is situated. Six cloaked figures sit in silence around a stone slab table, their faces hidden beneath shadowy cowls.

The table is full of what looks like half-eaten chickens. All that is recognisable are skeletal rib cages. The most beautiful dark silk covers the table, and, upon the cloth, are grand, etched carafes of red liquid. The others hail Tommy — Talon! — with tankards raised. He acknowledges them and accepts his place with a smile and a bow.

A wave of nausea washes through Tommy as the smells from the table reaches him. It is horrendous: rotten and metallic; sweet, yet mouldy.

These chicken carcasses are raw, thinks Tommy, before he realises what is being served. Not chicken, but human remains. Plates of butchered children, of half-eaten babies. Dread strikes Tommy and he tries to yell out, but he is frozen in terror. He tries to stop Talon —

himself — but he has no control of his dream. He is merely a voyeur, a passenger. He sees through Talon's eyes as he opens a large package on the table in front of him. From inside the wrapping, Daria looks at him through pleading, terrified eyes. Tommy thinks she is about to let out a scream. Talon grabs her by the throat, with one hand, whilst the sweeping finger-blades of his other hand decapitate her. Her head rolls on to the table and her neck stump pulses arterial spray. The hosts at the table laugh and cheer, but Tommy only sees Daria's innocent face. Pale, streaked with blood, and locked in an eternal look of betrayal. A trusting daughter callously murdered by her monstrous father.

Unaware of his macabre dreams, Daria feeds Tommy fish broth and freshly cooked black squirrel with honey. Although he never awakens, Tommy manages to keep the food down. After a couple of long nights, filled with feverish nightmares, Daria notices Tommy's energy start to return.

Tommy screams himself awake, clutching at his blanket, hellish visions ingrained on his retina like blood on silk. He hears the faint and distant laughter of a woman somewhere. The sound seems to come from behind him, from deep inside the ancient tunnels.

As he more fully awakens, sea air sifts through the shrouded cave entrance along with the sounds of the waves. The waves sound far calmer and more serene than those that greeted his arrival. Ever present seagulls, no doubt circling high above the cliffs, call out and their strangled voices intrigue Tommy's sluggish mind. These enticing sounds prompt his hurt body to investigate. He manages a fumbling crawl to the fabric camouflage door at the end of the cave — his first excursion from his rabbit-skin haven.

He pushes the entrance curtain aside and, as his light-deprived eyes adjust to naked sunlight, he is rewarded with a stunningly picturesque view.

NTB illusions could not create something so perfect, Tommy thinks.

Three-hundred feet up, the cave mouth overlooks the most perfect sunset he has ever seen. A noise to Tommy's left disturbs him. A friendly face appears. A dark-skinned woman smiles at him before whizzing down a zip-line and into a sea vessel — a grand sailboat of magnificent colours.

Vessels pepper the sea. All the boats — from large to small — are formed with the most exquisite artistry. Some are fierce-looking metal warships; some are wooden pirate galleons. There are long boats, catamarans, humble fishing boats and barges. There seem to be, arrayed before him, all the varieties of seafaring vehicles mankind could ever imagine. Nearest the cliffs he could even see dinghies, with children practising at the helm, bobbing around on the now still and calm sea. Looking to his right, he observes more people 'zipping' down lines to greet the diverse naval fleet.

There's a beautiful simplicity to the way these people live, thinks Tommy. The scene touches his heart, and he marvels at the fishing community life.

"Quite a sight, wouldn't you say?" says a familiar voice from above him.

A startled Tommy drops on all fours, painfully, and shuffles to the left of the entrance managing to twist and look up the cliff face. There he sees Talon, also on all fours, climbing headfirst towards him down the rough rock face.

To Tommy's amazement, the strange looking Talon is using his abnormal bone structure to cling to the rock face. Talon is carrying, secured to his back, a large bundle of wood and, dangling from a leather strap, tapping on his knotted forearms, are several plump birds and a couple of giant black squirrels.

Shuffling backwards out of the doorway, Tommy leaves the heavy camouflage material to one side, arranging a clear entrance for his surprising host.

Talon swings through the opening and lands silently and gracefully, despite his burdens. First, he discards the wood bundle and then, unclipping them from his huntsman belt, drops the dead animals on the cave floor. He walks across the cave, plops down cross-legged on his favourite seat — a low-set, comfortable-looking thing, covered in multicoloured furs — and smiles that haunting, plate-bone grin at Tommy. Still smiling, Talon pulls out several wooden bowls from beneath his seat. Talon adores his seat — and he tells this to Tommy on many occasions. Situated next to the cave wall, across from where the fire is located, it is in a prime position — the perfect spot for the cave's patriarch. He is obsessively protective of this seat for no real reason that Tommy can see, other than that it is his chair, and he likes it. Tommy finds this amusing — a demon, who lives in a cave, having an unrequited love affair with an armchair.

"You look better today; less shadow around your eyes," says Talon, as he unhooks a multi-coloured flask from his huntsman belt.

"Yeah.... I think I'm getting stronger," Tommy replies, cautiously studying Talon's decorated flesh and swordlike elbow spurs. This cave, the monstrosity before him, the lightning-quick (in more ways than one) child — they still seem unreal to Tommy. He still feels like none of this is really happening, everything here is surreal.

Talon throws the empty flask to Tommy.

"Here, fill it from there," Talon says, gesturing to a hidden alcove, two feet to the right of Tommy.

Feeling along the wall, Tommy's hand slips through camouflage rock material and into a stone alcove filled with ice-cold water. Shocked, he recoils and yelps. Noticing Talon's amused face, Tommy scowls and tries again, filling the flask.

"Sit, drink. Rest," Talon says.

Tommy takes a long pull from the flask and offers it back to Talon.

"No, keep it. I insist. Your flask was too small and awkward to carry, anyway. That there is a superior drinking vessel. Please, keep it. You've earned it for humouring me with your ridiculousness," Talon says still smiling that bizarre, slightly insane smile.

Tommy smiles back nervously.

"Thanks ... I guess. I've never been called ridiculous before. Oh well, I suppose there's a first time for everything." Tommy takes large gulps of the ice-cold water, thinking. He really doesn't see anything wrong with his own flask. But, as a guest — and a guest in significant debt to his hosts — he feels like he is in no position to disagree. Never insult a smiling blade-wielding devil. It seems a good rule to live by. *Live* being the operative word.

"The forest gives us life, little one. The shadows have flown from your eyes because the forest has healed you. It has absolved you of your destructive behaviour and, in its benevolence, restored you to full health." Talon says this in a mild and gentle manner. He points his long index blade at Tommy and inclines his head towards the haul of dead forest creatures.

Tommy just stares.

"I couldn't let you destroy any more of our hunting ground, young Tommy. Although, that is but one reason. There are many others."

Tommy wonders if Talon feels guilty. This thought makes Tommy uncomfortable, so he changes the topic. "From my perspective, you have an odd system of life. It seems valid. A direct and rewarding way to live. I would love to find out more about how this whole thing works." Tommy rubs his eyes, tired. Lights, sounds and conversation were now becoming a strain on his still quite fragile, healing body.

"Valid? Odd? These are words of a stupid person. We might have to change that," says Talon. He relaxes back into his chair and stretches his long arms above him, they creak like taut ship ropes.

"But I do feel that your clan's way of life is strange. I'm not stupid. I don't think I am, anyway." Tommy shuffled away from the cold draught at the cave-face towards where Talon sat, and the heat of the fire.

"I existed long before the Drumcroon facility sent innocent people to their deaths," Talon continues. "I have memories I can never really describe in words. Words are fragile, limited things. Ephemeral. They describe feelings, objects — things of immediacy. Things that exist in the now. They express a commonality, a shared frame of reference. When consciousness shifts so does the frame of reference, and words lose all meaning. They belong to a different realm of perspective. I originated in a place which is unexplainable in human terms. I have memories, if you can call them memories; and I remember where that place is, and how it feels to be there. Now I'm here talking to you, in this cave, and, yes, I'm calling you stupid. You have no idea where you are or what's happening. You are too intimidated to live but petrified to die. You are in a limbo state of constant fear. At night, in the woods, you would fear this little fellow." Talons flashes a serrated smile and holds out one of the large black squirrels. "A boogada boogada boo!" Talon says, launching the squirrel at Tommy. Without shifting his stare from Talon, Tommy plucks the dead creature out of the air. He throws the squirrel towards Talon's head and, this time, Talon catches it. The two stare at one another, Talon's plate-bone grin making soft grinding noises.

"How old are you, Talon? You look young," says Tommy, with a surprising lack of sarcasm.

"Your benevolence knows no bounds, kind soul," Talon sighs. He reaches for a dead forest bird. Grabbing clumps of its feathers, he starts quickly plucking the fowl.

"Can I help?"

"Set the fire, if you feel you have enough energy. That is, if you're not too scared of what's back there, in the dark."

Concern flashes on Tommy's face as he notices for the first time his bare right arm. How could he not have noticed it before?

"Where are my joining tools?"

"The fever made them detach from you."

"I want them back."

"They're safe."

"I need them, Talon. They're all I have now. They are everything to me."

Talon sighs. "I would prefer you to stay like this for a while. As you are my guest, in my home, you have become my responsibility."

Tommy struggles to his feet, then falls. Talon catches him before he hits the ground.

"You're still weak," Talon says, as he lowers him. "Youth betrays you, makes you believe the power you wield is everything, and eternal. You're too unstable to understand the truth. What you possess is useless without control. You can't have control without knowing who, or what, you are. You must suffer for wisdom. True gnosis and pain are intricately woven, like the strongest of sea ropes." Talon puts Tommy to bed, like a naughty child, and returns to his favourite seat. Tommy, although unsettled, tries to find comfort by pulling one of the fur blankets, ubiquitous in the cave, about his sore shoulders.

One of Talon's fingers rips through the plucked bird's ribcage and he swiftly moves his index blade the full length of the dead bird, opening its chest cavity. The insides he removes by using the sides of two sharp fingers. Talon dumps the innards into one of the hand-carved wooden bowls without spilling a drop onto the cave's ancient floor. The foul stink of the internal organs hits Tommy. It makes his nose sting with the bird's hidden rot. The smell crawls down to his throat, making his gore rise. Tommy clamps a hand over his mouth and nose — to stop his stomach contents rising to meet the stench — but he cannot stop himself from watching the butchery skills with a nauseated curiosity. Seeing Talon working hard to feed him, Tommy feels the need to say some words of thanks. Perhaps kind words would also be medicine for his broken and vulnerable condition. He wants to thank Talon for his kindness, but a certain paranoid fear inside him wonders if, one day, Talon's butchery skills may yet be used on him.

"You saved my life. I understand that the joining tools bother you and, as long as they are safe, I'm happy to obey your rules. I find myself indebted to you and your family for saving my life."

"Remember the day; remember the deed," says Talon. "You have a great future if you can keep this attitude. We share similar traits, me and you. I believe that your soul will not fall into the abyss. You could possess what it takes to survive, given time. You will learn, or you will lose your head".

Talon uses two of his fingers in a scissor action to remove the head and legs of the plump wood pigeon, then he moves on to the next bird.

The finger blades Talon possesses fascinate Tommy. And, not for the first time, Tommy thinks: *He's terrifying. Horrific. He cannot get any scarier.*

Until this moment Tommy had lived a rather sheltered existence. A clean, mostly blood-free existence. Tommy's family and the Guardians had shielded him from the truth of this harsh world, concealing him like the internal stink of intestines. Tommy searches his mind for experiences, for reference points — anything to process these smells, these sights, these sounds. His senses expand, invisible tendrils snaking out and demanding reference markers from his tired brain; but nothing is there. The sights, sounds and smells are new, real — and shockingly alien. He tries and fails to rationalise the scene as 'merely a horned demon mutilating a squirrel,' but his brain just does not accept the description. He realises that it is not Talon that is making him uneasy, it is the realness — the rawness — of this experience. *The NTB learning pods at the Drumcroon facility are not programmed to simulate this level of reality*, thinks Tommy.

"The fires not going to build itself, young Tommy," Talon says, interrupting Tommy's musing.

"Oh. Right. Okay, yeah ... Er ...I — I don't know how to do it without my tools."

Talon stops plucking the second wood pigeon and smiles at Tommy. Tommy once more takes in the detail of Talon's upper and lower masses of serrated bone, that lie below his spike of a nose. The lethality of his smile is obvious. Tommy finds himself wondering how many throats it has torn out, how many defending hands it has bitten in half. Talon's smile radiates the same menace heard in the sound of an ancient warrior determinedly drawing his sword from its scabbard.

What kind of hellish place spawns a creature such as this? thinks Tommy.

"I suppose there are many things we can learn from one another," says Talon.

Tommy returns the fearsome smile with one less lethal, less interesting.

Talon moves to the back of the cave, climbs up the wall, and returns with a brown hessian sack. He pulls dried leaves from the bag and piles them up inside the fire's circle of stones.

Talon strikes the edge of two of his finger blades together, scraping off a shower of sparks which start to smoke and smoulder in the nest of kindling. Crouching low, Talon blows on the embers until flames take hold. Tommy feels that he should show some initiative, and shuffles to the woodpile, hauling out a thick branch.

"No, No," Talon corrects, "the delicate twigs."

"Like this?" Tommy says, snapping off delicate branches.

"Good, good, the thin ones," Talon says. "Once they catch, slowly build up to thicker ones." Talon leaves the fire to Tommy and returns to dressing the game.

Tommy blows and blows under the leaves, mimicking Talon, and the flames curl around the small twigs, they crackle and spit. A question bursts from Tommy and, no sooner as he says it, he instantly feels stupid.

"How old are you, Talon?"

Talon pauses in his plucking, smirking. Tommy is painfully aware of the intrusiveness of his blunt question as the silence grows — then relief, as Talon replies.

"How old would you think me, young Tommy?"

"I — I'm sorry, Talon, I couldn't say."

"The fire is going out. Keep blowing on the sticks and add some bigger ones."

"Okay."

"I know what you're thinking."

"What?" Tommy says.

"You think that it's hard to tell how old I am because of my strange appearance, yes?"

"I, well, I *was* thinking..."

"It's fine, Tommy. I have an appearance considered by many to be ... Odd, perhaps? I, however, see it as a gift. And sometimes —" Talon stops plucking and stares out of the entrance of the cave. He studies the moving clouds in the darkening sky, then he looks thoughtfully at his bladed hands — "Sometimes, a curse. Yes, it is a curse, to some extent."

Then, his reflection period over, Talon's lethal fingers deftly snips off the head and feet of a bird — the extremities landing neatly in separate bowls.

"I've seen more seasons pass by than I care to remember."

"So — are you much older than my father? He's fifty-six and —"

"Don't you dare speak of your father to me, boy!" Talon thunders. His deep-set, horn-rimmed eyes of dark coal somehow seem to burn with ancient flames.

Tommy startles and has no time to mask his shock.

"Let's change the subject," Talon says, snatching up a black squirrel and taking a deep steadying breath. "We were talking of my age, yes?"

"Sorry, Talon, yes, we were," Tommy says, glad of the conversational change as the tension in the air drops markedly.

"We will start with Daria. It's easier to explain things this way."

Talon stares into the dead squirrel's face a moment and gently strokes the soft black fur on its head, with a thoughtful smile now returning to his fiendlike face.

"You know her to be three, right? And she is, to me, anyway. To you, though, she would be three times seven years of age."

"Twenty-one," Tommy calculates with no thought. Talon meets his confused stare and nods.

"Twenty-one?" Tommy repeats with mounting disbelief.

"In what you class as a year, she has seen twenty-one of those," Talon says, holding Tommy's shocked stare as Tommy gently touches his still-healing facial wounds.

"She's clever," Tommy blurts out, rather randomly, smiling and shaking his head.

"She is," Talon says.

"Twenty-one," Tommy says to himself, backing away from the growing heat of the fire. He throws larger pieces into the centre of the stone circle and then sits on a comfortable fur blanket.

"Yes, twenty-one. But to me, she is three."

"And you, Talon?" Tommy's curiosity, in harmony with the progress of the fire, builds to a blaze.

"As you reckon it, I would be more like one hundred and sixty-eight times seven years," Talon says.

Tommy's mouth falls open. "You're one thousand, one hundred and seventy-six years old?"

Talon nods, still smiling. He guts the big black squirrel and then peels off its skin, like peeling a bloody banana.

"Approximately, yes. Although, I prefer to be considered one hundred and sixty-eight. That is in my years."

"How is that possible?" asks Tommy.

"As I said, young Tommy, we have a lot to learn from one another."

Bewildered, the only thing that comes into Tommy's mind to say to the horned demon in a cave who is preparing a meal for him is, "You look remarkably young for your age." The words come out in a voice that is weak and croaky. His mouth and throat feel dehydrated from blowing the flames, so he finds the multi-coloured, leather flask Talon gave him and drinks deeply from it.

Talon goes behind his seat and pulls out yet another wooden bowl. This one is three times the size of the other vessels, which are filled with feathers and offal.

"Fill it from the alcove and wash your hands and face," Talon recommends as he passes over the bowl, followed by a sea sponge and a rough fabric drying cloth. He drags a few pieces of metal over to the fire and slots the two birds and squirrel through some spits. He throws several logs onto the fire and says that, when this wood is burnt down, the spits will be put up. Feverish and sticky nights had made Tommy's eyelids gummy and heavy. The water is cold and refreshing. After Tommy finishes his ablutions, he notices Talon at the cave mouth, his arms outstretched.

"Talon?" Tommy asks in quiet confusion.

"I should also wash before eating," says Talon, over his left shoulder, before diving out of sight.

Tommy scrambles over to where Talon was, only seconds earlier. Shaking his head, Tommy sees, three hundred feet below, Talon swimming in the sea. Laughter erupts from multiple cavern entrances all along the cliff face.

Tommy laughs, too, as Talon gives him a wave from among the many bobbing boats.

"That's nothing," says a booming voice near Tommy. A mountain of a man emerges from nowhere. The cave gives birth to his bulk, and he jumps — plummeting with no grace, but massive force, into the water. There is an explosion as he hits the sea followed by the hysterical laughter of children, as the small boats they are in rock violently, and a tidal wave of water soaks them.

Talon leaps on the giant man's back. The whale-like man circles around the giggling children's boats, underwater, as Talon stands on his back. The children poke at the large man, who seems not to need air, with oars and other items and shout, "Thankwell! Thankwell!"

To the assembled children's joy, Thankwell surfaces to blow a spray of water into their faces. Thrusting forth an imaginary harpoon, Talon shouts out, "I am Ahab. I am Ahab. I have caught the great, white whale!"

Despite not knowing who or what an 'Ahab' is, Tommy finds the rising laughter infectious. He shouts down, "Get him, Ahab! Get him!"

It takes Tommy three months to completely heal from his many injuries. During this time, his strange new friends initiate him into their clan. Tommy is a part of a new community of people: he is a part of the northern coast cliff clan. In the clan, everyone calls him Astilla. When he asks what it means, Daria says nothing, but the others say: "Astilla is your clan-name."

Tommy is accepted by Talon, who is the founder and leader of the clan. Daria gives Tommy his clan-name. Pandeminia, the name-giver of the clan, is nearing the end of her life, and Daria, her long-time apprentice, is her natural successor. Tutored by Pandeminia, Daria nurtures the gift of finding the *other* inside of people. Talon explains this to Tommy in elementary terms:

"There is the name a person is born with — the name which holds no substance to who they are, the adult they evolve into — and then there is, hidden inside, the person's *other* name. This other name is an amalgamation of who you are and the path you are on. The other name defines what you truly are — who you will become. It is important to the clan folk that they have a name which reflects their true nature."

Tommy has many talks with Talon. Talon admits his original plan was to live amongst the prisoners because he wanted a new life away from the endless regulations of the Drumcroon facility. Talon's advice is instrumental in Tommy's decision to leave this wonderful place: "You should continue with your plans. It's your path. Everybody needs to stick to their own trail." Tommy rarely takes advice from anyone, but, looking at Talon, he could tell this strange man has a wisdom that was deep and far-reaching.

Tommy's time in the cavern on the northern coast of the island, surrounded by prison planet Earth's oldest community is his first true learning curve. Tommy learns the basics of sailing from Thankwell. When he is misunderstood, Thankwell's temper is volcanic; and Tommy constantly misunderstands Thankwell. The cause of Tommy's continued confusion is Thankwell's limited vocabulary, especially when technical sailing matters are discussed. In the beginning of Thankwell's essential teachings, the big man is silent. He uses small hand signals and grunts and, when these hand signals and grunts are inevitably not understood, Thankwell grabs Tommy by an arm and leg, and launches him into the water, skimming him across the ocean. It is in these moments — when Tommy finds himself skipping across the surface of the sea like an oddly-shaped, screaming pebble — that the inspiration to learn fast, and try harder, finally manifests itself. Thankwell often heads back to the caves alone, leaving Tommy to drown or make the journey back to land successfully. It was this kind of 'tough love' training which made Tommy's body strong, his mind quick, and his mouth, more-often-than-not firmly shut.

CHAPTER SIX

Sailing with Thankwell

Strange how paranoia can link up with
reality now and then.

-Philip K. Dick-

6

Learning to sail is a painful experience for Tommy. In addition to taking on the tumultuous and chaotic ocean, his teacher, Thankwell, is an equally unpredictable force of nature. Tommy's nerves are in tatters as the huge man steps onto the craft. The craft — a dual-hulled catamaran called Boomer — creaks in protest and sways on the water's surface. Thankwell's Boomer is etched in intricate carvings that depict moments in the strange life of this water giant.

The engravings are fascinating. Tommy spends many hours trying to interpret these hieroglyphs; to turn them into a workable story. Many of the carvings are unmistakably Talon. There are several depictions of women, one of which looks pregnant. Fresher carvings show Thankwell under the sea surrounded by strange underwater towers. Tommy thinks these ancient buildings must be those the sea has claimed back after the meteorite strike of 4423AD, when the world changed into this ocean planet, killing the millions who could not afford transport off world.

Thankwell's boat is covered in gems and semi-precious stones, like a whale encrusted with barnacles: Trinkets lost to time and the ocean; mechanisms attached in decorative mandalas; runes on the higher parts of the hull and in bands on the main mast, and small oceanic maps carved into the beams. In the full glare of the sun, the gems and pearls, shells and trinkets, glint and sparkle. Tommy feels spellbound by the craft. Unfortunately, this reverie is often interrupted by being smashed around the head by the swinging boom of the craft, as Thankwell tacks downwind. The boom of Thankwell's well-named craft frequently causes Tommy headaches. It is easy to get distracted by Boomer: the carvings on its ornately etched wood hold him entranced with their mysteries. An engineer by inclination and training, Tommy gravitates towards puzzles. Between lessons with Thankwell, and in lulls in conversation (if such an accusation could ever be levelled at the practically mute behemoth), he slowly starts to piece the story together that, if Tommy is correct, is truly amazing.

Some of the carvings depict Thankwell diving to the very lowest levels of the ocean, to research the ancient ruins, recording his elaborate findings on the surfaces of this boat. The boat is both research vessel and lab book.

The initial sailing lessons Tommy found to be straightforward. Thankwell points to the front of the boat and announces, "Bow." *Okay*. He points to the back of the boat and says, "Stern." *Fine*. Facing the bow, and pointing to the right side of the boat, he says, "Starboard." *Sure*. Still facing the bow, he points to the left side of the boat and says, "Port." *Right*. The vertical and longest piece of wood is pointed out as, "Mast." *Obviously*. The horizontal wood coming from the mast is identified: "Boom." *Makes sense*.

Thankwell's lesson now moves to the sails, which is what attracted Tommy to these fascinating crafts in the first place. There are three sails: mainsail, jib and spinnaker. The mainsail harnesses the wind to provide the main driving power; the jib — the smallest of the sails —

provides balance and is utilised for tacking, moving side-to-side across waves; and the spinnaker — the middle-sized sail — is used for sailing downwind. Thankwell points out the top of the sails as "Head," the bottom as "Foot," and the sides as "Luff" and "Leach" — Tommy will always mix those two up.

Thankwell licks his finger and holds it up, testing the wind's direction. Tommy copies him. The sailing lecture concludes as Thankwell points in the direction the wind is blowing *to*, downwind, and says, "Leeward," then points towards where the wind was blowing *from* and says, "Windward." He looks around the panoramic sea view, as if seeing things Tommy cannot — which, of course, he can. "Now watch," Thankwell says. "Learn."

Thankwell takes Tommy out on the water for one or two hours each day, and only in pleasant weather, building up his experience slowly. Occasional shorter trips are carried out in less clement weather. After one stormy trip, Thankwell returns carrying a half-drowned Tommy. Unconscious for an entire day, he spends the next three days recovering.

The storm is all Tommy can see in his mind's eye. At night, as the veil of darkness surrounds him, his sleeping consciousness returns to the swell of those dark waters — the toppling of *Boomer*. In his nightmares, Thankwell laughs at him as he drowns. He can see the giant's mouth: larger than normal, stretched wide and full of teeth — rows of shark teeth gleam. During these days of recuperation, through the night terrors, Daria is ever vigilant, watching over him.

Daria's anger at Thankwell grows, like an ignored boil. To Talon's evident amusement, Daria goes next door to let Thankwell have a piece of her mind. She screams at Thankwell and runs around the brute in a blur, aiming slaps at him which Thankwell cannot hope to deflect, like a tiny fly buzzing around a quarter-ton buffalo.

"Everything Thankwell's Fault! All the time! Astilla never listens to Thankwell! This what happens when you don't listen!" Thankwell shouts after a long-gone Daria.

After Daria's admonishment — and assault — Thankwell disappears.

"He does this every time I tell him off," Daria explains. "He'll sulk for a while — like the big baby he is! — then he'll come back with a gift for you, when he's thought about his behaviour."

Daria is right. A week later, Thankwell stoops into the cave and sits for a while staring at Tommy — who is hiding under his covers like a small child, terrified. From his haven, Tommy notices that Thankwell's mouth is not like it is in his nightmares. His teeth are hidden. His hair is free from seaweed. His appearance is altogether less monstrous. There is something in Thankwell's hand, wrapped in hessian.

"Here. This is for you. She belongs you, now. She keep you safe," Thankwell says in a low rumble. He places the hessian bundle on Tommy's bed, gently pats a cowering Tommy on the head and walks away.

"If you weak, you eaten. Everything eats everything," says Thankwell softly from the cave mouth. "Don' be weak, Astilla. Don' get eaten."

Then Thankwell is gone.

Tommy waits. There is the inevitable, booming splash of impact and Tommy hears faint cheers from the children in the bay below. They seem inordinately fond of this frightful man. Their laughter is mixed with the caws of the gulls and other quotidian sounds of life. Tommy slowly picks at the rope around the brown hessian bundle. Unbinding the package, he reveals a sturdy looking black leather belt with a built-in scabbard. Protruding from the sheath is a whalebone hilt, inlaid with mother of pearl. Tommy pulls the hilt, revealing a sea knife of unparalleled beauty. He studies the detailed whalebone handle. Illustrations are etched in fine needle-point detail — black lines that are sealed with a lacquer that makes the handle shine. The pictures show a rough sea and Tommy navigating a Catamaran solo through the storm. The sea and the sky seem to fuse into one in the storm's whirling maelstrom. The sky and sea are stylistically depicted in a decorative knot-work motif. Beneath the boat, under the water, Thankwell, is wrestling a giant squid. *Perhaps it is just Thankwell getting his tea?* thinks Tommy. *I must ask him. No, maybe not. Thankwell's not really the explanation type. I'll ask Daria. She's close to Thankwell, despite their tiffs from time to time.*

Tommy has no clue how something so intricate and fine can be made by someone like Thankwell. The blade shimmers in the light, with swirls of green and blue running through the middle. It is razor sharp and looks ideal for cutting ropes and gutting fish. Its blade is long, with serrations on the back. Tommy slides the knife reverentially back into its sheath and fastens on the belt. A new sense of pride washes over him as he admires it — it is a beautiful gift.

Later that evening, Thankwell visits again with two lengths of rope. He passes one rope to Tommy and they spend a few hours practicing knots.

Tommy watches the giant, and the giant looks back. Thankwell does not look at the rope, hands working independently, as he makes the first knot of many. A knot can save your life, but only if you can do it in the dark, with wet, slippery rope on a boat rising and falling like a rollercoaster. In short, your hands need to do them automatically, without thinking.

"Thumb knot," Thankwell states, showing it to Tommy — the knot dwarfed by his huge, ham fists. Tommy watches intently as knots form and dissolve under the deceptively nimble fingers of the huge man. By the end of the session, Tommy remembers all that Thankwell has shown him. He demonstrates his knowledge on his own stretch of rope, forming various types: the overhand, or thumb, knot; the square knot;

the figure of eight; the bowline; the clove hitch, and the double half hitch.

Thankwell has a surprised look on his face as Tommy proceeds. Thankwell's jaw lowers as Tommy blazes through the knots with the speed and skill only a time-served mariner should possess. Thankwell's shocked gape turns into a wide, open-mouthed grin, showing Tommy two things.

Thankwell's pointed teeth have more than one layer, reducing in size from front to back, row after row, teeth jostling for position and, shark-like, rear ones moving forward to replace those lost in front. The second thing Tommy notes is that Thankwell is genuinely impressed. Thankwell simply says, "Good. Tomorrow I show you what use when." Thankwell grabs Tommy's knot rope and uses a square knot to join the two ropes together and throws it back to Tommy. "Practice. Knots save lives."

Tommy is impressed with his progress, and happy there is a lighter side to this fascinating, if scary, giant.

Thankwell is as good as his word and, the very next morning, he goes through every knot from the previous night and explains their uses. With knots familiarised, Thankwell takes Tommy on longer trips out in *Boomer*. The island that Tommy has lived on his entire life looks like a little, insignificant, black dot on the undulating horizon. Tommy is still nervous around Thankwell, though, and, maybe because of this, his mistakes start to increase again.

The large sea mariner possesses jaws that Tommy can imagine biting arms, heads, legs off. Despite his wariness, Tommy mimics Thankwell's actions well, and the big man soon warms to the young man. Eventually, Thankwell grudgingly admits that Tommy can sail solo, with at least *some* confidence and awareness of danger.

The final great gift from this wonderful community is a sleek-looking, one-berth catamaran donated by the expert craftsman Rhombus. Rhombus tells Tommy that the craft is called Slash, because of the clean way the two blades of its multihull cut through the water. Rhombus boasts that this boat could top 20 knots, and — weather and pilot permitting — should make the 300-mile sea journey to the Lanes, on the far side of the island, in less than 12 hours.

Daria waves goodbye to Tommy with tears flowing down her cheeks, smothered in Talon's lethal, but protective, arms.

"Goodbye, Astilla. Please be safe. Come back to see us again...I'll miss you!"

Tommy smiles.

"Please, Daria, what does the name Astilla mean? It's driving me mad. I need to know."

Talon smiles down at his daughter as she goes shy, burying her head into his chest.

"In your language, it means 'splinter'," she shouts into Talon's leathery chest.

"It's perfect, Daria. Thank you. I thank you from the bottom of my heart for fixing me when I couldn't fix myself, when I was broken. I will return with great treasures. Treasures fit for a princess — princess Daria!" Shouts Tommy, with a grand flourish.

Tommy stares at the scars on his left arm and absently, with his right hand, he touches his face, the raised scars on the left cheek. He runs his hand through his hair as the wind fills the mainsail.

Tommy's adopted family continue to wave at him as he fades into the distance — as he sets sail on calm water to a different life, an unpredictable expanse stretching out as far as the dark sea travels — into the unknown.

"What great treasures will he get me, Papa?" Daria asks, beaming at Talon. Talon turns from his happy daughter to pointedly look at Thankwell — who sighs, scratches his head and rubs his eyes. He knows what that look means.

"I doin' it, I doin' it," says Thankwell, walking into the sea.

"Where's he going? Am I really a princess, Papa?" Daria asks as Talon sweeps her up into his arms.

"You're more akin to a goddess, my darling," he smiles. "Don't worry about Thankwell. He is unpredictable these days. Who knows what's inside that big hollow head of his? Maybe it's just like his mouth, filled with teeth — teeth that bite!"

"I think his head is full of fishhooks and seaweed," says Daria.

They both laugh.

Tommy turns to the sea; his friends fast becoming specks in the distance behind him. Thoughts fill his head. He remembers Talon's whispered advice, so as not to wake a sleeping Daria, last night, as he handed Tommy back his dangerous joining tools:

"...Keep to the ocean, about a mile off the coast. Let the strong easterly wind take you all the way West to the Lanes, on the far side of this rock. Do not — I repeat, do *not* — set foot in the Barrens. It belongs to those who live under it, the Barrenites. They have no remorse, no pity — and they kill as freely as we breathe. Our coastal cliff clans stay clear of the Barrenite's territory and the Barrenites, in return, leave us to our ways. Fierce wars were once fought over these boundaries, but now we live in a time of peace. It is a precarious peace — but it is peace, nonetheless. If either of us were to break the terms of our peace, and trespass on agreed territories, it would lead to all-out war. So, Tommy, please stick to the ocean, and try to stay about a mile from the coast. Take no risks."

"What are these Barrenites? Where do they come from?" Tommy asked.

Daria stirred, letting out a whimper. Talon looked over towards his sleeping daughter and then, when she no longer moved, back to Tommy.

"They will tear you apart. They hate, they kill, they taste blood, they go into rages, and they don't stop. It's no time to be telling great stories of perilous times, long past. Just stick to the sea, a mile from the coast."

Tommy noticed, at this moment, how vacant Talon's eyes became. Talon stared deep into the flames, as if communing with the plasma. Lost in memory and fire. Lost in blood and war.

"Talon, are you alright?" Tommy whispered.

Talon shook away his memories and said, "Stick to the sea. Soon you will be back among others who come from your world. I cannot promise that everything will be just as it should, but you will regain a footing on the troublesome path that you have chosen as your way of life. Astilla, your road will be hard, your soul is going to be swimming in pain. I have seen such sights — such a terrible trail, such violent ends." There is no bitterness in Talon's voice, only the distant thoughtfulness of a man who has lived a long, long time.

"Yes, that's why I've come prepared, Talon. I have —"

"Yes, yes, I know, the magic arm," Talon said.

"Yeah. That's going to keep me safe," replied Tommy, a little defensively.

"If you insist," said Talon.

"I know you think I'm useless, Talon — but I'm not. I can look after myself. I don't need anyone. I'm self-contained and, if these Barrenites show up, well, I... I'll prove myself in combat." Tommy looked from the fire to Talon.

Talon's eyes pierced Tommy as if he were staring into his soul. Tommy felt a shiver run down his spine.

"If you kill one of these creatures then do not stop. Execute every single one you see. Because, if you leave any witnesses, word will spread to those below the earth. There are real demons on this island, Astilla, and they don't need a magic arm to do their carnage. They're born to murder. There are things beneath us, things that are unspeakable, things that turn even my stomach. Creatures I have fought before, in the tunnels throughout this land, tunnels I helped to dig centuries ago. If the pact between our two communities is broken it will result in a terrible war. I will have to fight, once more, and when I kill..." Talon leaned back, put his hands behind his head and sighed, the sentiment unfinished.

"I do not fear demons that hide in caves and tunnels," said Tommy. He remembered holding Talon's gaze — not an easy thing to do.

"You do what you will, young Tommy," Talon said with an intensity which was unsettling. "This is all pointless. I should have realised warning a young hero such as yourself would be foolish. Trees tremble to pieces in your presence, do they not? But I — I, Tommy, actually miss battle. I do. I miss everything about battle: the screams, the missing limbs, the blood; terrified souls calling for their mothers, covered in their friends' intestines; the screams, the pleadings, the bite of my blades, the gurgling death."

"I might not engage them in combat, though. It depends," said Tommy, his voice shaking slightly.

"I would advise, Tommy — and you need not heed it, it's your path, after all — that you stick to the sea. It's the only way you will reach your destination alive. You might want to go ashore and inspect these strange creatures, these colourful oddities. I can see that about you. You have a curiousness inside of you, a questing nature. But, if you go to the Barrens, you die."

"You misjudge me, Talon."

"No, you misjudge the Barrenites," said Talon. "Look, it's late. Tomorrow you leave this place, for a life of adventure. This is your last night of protection and safety. Take advantage of these peaceful hours and rest, for tomorrow you sail to your destiny, Astilla of the northern clifftop coastal clan. Whatever you choose that destiny to be."

At first, Tommy heeds Talon's advice, mindful of the danger of the terrible creatures that lurk under the Barrens. Unfortunately, Tommy's curiosity always conquers his fear. Looking to catch a glimpse of these odd creatures, his catamaran drifts closer to the shore. Tommy's self-inflicted injuries had, perhaps, temporarily numbed his appetite for adventure. Only now — as he skips over the waves, the wind in his hair, watching the cliffs and small beaches speed by — does he feel his lust for adventure return. A certain burden lifts from Tommy. The open water, the sounds of the gulls and the cloudless sky bathe him with a kind light. The wind is steady in his sail and he barely feels motion as Slash spears through the water. He closes his eyes, and takes in the feel of the ocean, as the waves purl about his bows.

His joining tools are in a stitched backpack that Talon gave him. Tommy is also wearing the magnificent sea knife and belt that Thankwell had made for him. He feels secure, safe in the knowledge that he has allies nearby.

Seven miles down the coast, and moving at speed, Tommy's concentration is distracted by three dark shapes ambling up the narrow and rocky shore to his left. So intrigued is Tommy by the movement of these mysterious shapes, he does not notice Slash drifting landwards.

On the shore are a family of black bears, two smaller cubs trailing behind their mother. The mother bear stops and sniffs the air, her nose moving up and down like a striking fisherman's rod. Tommy glides over towards the bears. He drops the sails, gently drifting, so he can observe these amazing creatures.

The cumbersome mother bear suddenly springs into life and bolts into the sea, with surprising agility she plunges into the waves, surfacing with a large crab in her jaws. Repositioning the crab to the rear of her mouth, she chomps down with her carnassials. Even from where he is, Tommy can hear the crack of the crab's carapace. The mother bear drops the lifeless creature to the sandy shore, where her cubs bounce over to it, happily nipping at each other, excited to feed. It is at that moment that the mother black bear notices Tommy. She meets his curious stare and returns a curious gaze of her own, rising on her back legs and snuffling the air. Realising there is no real threat from this boat and its occupant, she returns her attention to the cubs that are fighting over parts of the crab.

Her own hunger ignored for the sake of her offspring, Tommy thinks. *Fascinating.*

As he looks upon the great bear, she rears onto her back legs again, and looks around the narrow rocky shore, smelling for hidden signals in the air. Tommy follows her stare down the long thin beach and notices what has attracted the huge black bear's attention. A solitary lynx slightly further down the beach is trying in vain to drag a large dead seal towards the cliffs, away from the approaching bears. The mother bear briefly looks towards her cubs, and, seeing no immediate threats to them, she chases off the much smaller predator. The lynx quickly releases the seal, grabs a detached flipper in its mouth, and gracefully pounces up onto a low cliff ledge. From this safe vantage point, it watches the fierce bear lumbering up the beach, spraying water behind it as it runs through tidepools. Slowing now it closes on the seal carcass, the bear myopically eyes the ledge-bound lynx and grunts at it.

Tommy laughs at the scene. He compares the bear's stature to Thankwell, but its attitude is more like fearsome little Daria. Tommy considers the lynx: maybe a little smarter, but wary of the bear's might. Who is the lynx? Him, perhaps?

Tommy would have loved to spend all day watching the bears make their way down the narrow coast and getting into adventures, but he is aware of something. A feeling more than anything — a feeling that something in the nearby trees is watching him. Watching him like he was watching the bears and the lynx.

His smile wilting, paranoia growing, he raises the mainsails and the dual-hulls of the catamaran cuts through the steady waters once more — bouncing gently over the waves and powering Tommy away. His attention is firmly focused on the cliff tops now. A further feeling of being watched tickles at the back of his brain.

The uneasy feeling remains for two miles, five miles — ten miles. A voice inside his mind whispers to him of hideous seeking eyes and hungry drooling mouths.

The shore widens, from narrow rocky bays to the enticing, golden inlets of sandy beaches. These sun-coloured oases are only interrupted by the dark fang-like rocks protruding seaward from forested cliffs of granite located more inland.

A female voice screams. The shrill noise sends fear jolting through Tommy. The lone scream is joined by more screams and now scared voices are recognisable: men and women calling for help. The voices grow still clearer as Slash shoots onward. The treeline ends and a large clearing is visible. Stone tables and plinths surround its perimeter. Dark shapes move within the trees and things emerge from the woods at every edge of the clearing.

A hooded figure with hooded followers emerges from the tree line, their lethal, spindly-looking arm-claws stretched towards the sky in some form of supplication. Tommy wants to move, but he is frozen with fear. The priestly leader is surrounded by half-naked, twisted figures. They circle him, howling and chanting, spinning wildly. They are dancing mutants —twisted, hellish — real life monsters. Their knees bend backwards, their spines protrude from their backs in a bony shield. The hooded priest figure looks over this congregation with obvious excitement, and the deformed gang of hellish beasts are flagellating one another using long branches, or simple switches.

Tommy stares in shock, in disgust, breathing heavily.

Leave, Tommy thinks. *Keep away from them. Continue down the coast, one mile from the shore. This is not your fight.*

The leader's arms raise, calming this group of freaks. There is an eerie silence — waves seem to freeze, birds seem to hang in the sky, their chattering silenced. The cool sea breeze buffeting Tommy starts to turn warm and takes on a sulphurous smell.

The demons on the clifftop silence everything with their presence — all natural order, all harmony, is corrupted by their unnatural nature. The birds circling overhead are the only witnesses to the clifftop speech from a cloaked figure.

Tommy is still too far away — or, perhaps, not far enough away — his curiosity is now fuelling his boldness to get closer and, in doing so, break his promise to Talon.

"Stay a mile from the coast, let the breeze take you down the coast to the Lanes, to your own kind," whispers Tommy mockingly to himself, remembering Talon's advice.

Closer to the cliff face now. Four more hooded figures appear, dragging people out from the woods.

Tommy recognises the clothing as the grey and green uniforms of cadets. He had helped bundle many prisoners, like these, into holding cells to await their banishment. As the cries of the cadets reach him, on the choking air around the cliffs, all he wants to do is sail away; to just turn around and imagine this is just another disturbing NTB illusion.

Tommy wants to call out to them — to help — but no noise issues from his pale, bloodless lips. Tommy just stares, wordlessly mouthing words, as screams start to come once more from the terrified cadets. Something deep inside Tommy's soul screams. Adrenaline surges and, finally spurred into action, he shifts the boom and directs the boat landwards, trying to reach the cliffs as fast as possible. Up on the clifftop, the cadets are one by one being thrown to the beasts.

Tommy releases a scream of his own now — a scream of pure horror. Plumes of blood fountain, screams turn to bloody gurgles, monster's teeth and claws rend them limb from limb.

It is a scene of mass butchery the likes of which Tommy has never experienced. Tommy's face is drawn into a mask of rage and something shudderingly powerful stirs within him. Within range now, he attaches the joining tools to his right arm, attaches the MechVision to his left eye. Snaking vein-like implants flash angrily under his skin. The excruciating pain from attaching the tool to both his eye socket and arm simultaneously knocks Tommy to his knees for a moment. Clutching his head, he feels the swarming of a thousand wasps, stinging, trying to burst from the top of his skull. Tommy's eyes flash as a luminous violet energy shoots across his pupils. The power of the EPC is surging through him, now, and he gains control of the energy, reacquainting himself with its thrumming energies. Pointing the lethal device at the carnage unfolding on the summit of the cliff, he finds his voice.

"Seeker arrows: FIRE!"

Five bolts of golden technology blast towards the horrors on the clifftop as they bite, rip, and tear screams (and more) from the cadets. A golden ribbon flows from the joining rods to the streaking golden arrows, which slam into five different beasts. The monsters yelp with shock, but the arrows have yet to deliver their full payment. To the mutants' mounting horror, the arrows begin to change shape inside of them. The former arrows are now golden claws, moving inside the foul beast's bodies, clutching what they can ...a tibia... a rib... an ankle bone... a skull.

One hand clutches a monster's spinal column, instantly paralysing it. The four hooded figures, at the back of the massacre, mimic their leader's surprise at seeing their kin attacked.

Confused, the cloaked figures lower their hoods to reveal their grotesque faces: translucent jelly-like flesh, disjointed jaws which open like flower petals and, inside their drooling mouths, hundreds of needle-sharp teeth — useless for tearing flesh but perfect for latching onto a severed limb. The black, spider-like eyes of these beasts show no emotion as they pull long blades from their sleeves. Below the cliff, Tommy's arm is still pointing at the cliff face — at the murderers.

"Cowards!" yells Tommy, ripping back his modified arm, and, with it, the five attached monsters. The leader attempts to grab his brethren, but claws at only fresh air.

Tommy finds a strange pleasure in the confusion displayed on this monster's face, as the carnivorous congregation soar off the cliff to their doom. The disgust on the leader's face is obvious as he climbs over the dead and dying cadets to see his clan dead — their broken bodies strewn on the seaweed-covered boulders below.

Tommy winces at the horrific sight of mangled limbs and spilled innards on the shore. The misshapen head of the leader looks down from the clifftop and screams something unintelligible. Tommy is now thirty feet from the cliff face, he strains to hear what the rasping voice of this beast is saying, but he is still too distant.

"You carry on ranting, I'll be with you in a minute, you ugly bastard!" Tommy shouts back.

He shines a violet light over the now returned Seeker Arrows, tainted, though they are, with bits of the yellowing monster flesh and dark red blood. Tommy bangs the back of his blast boots against the mast of the catamaran, freeing his serrated boot blades, then changes the arrows of his right arm into a large, circular cannon. Two golden cables unravel, from the side of the newly formed air cannon, and two silver foot braces appear. Standing in the braces he aims the air cannon towards the water and fires. A blast of continuous air shoots him up, over the water, and slams him into the cliff face. In Tommy's haste, he has misread the trajectory.

Tommy clings to the cliff, face lacerated and left shoulder damaged on the jagged cliff rocks. Blood flowing freely, heart pounding, the smell from the disembowelled monsters below wafts up towards him. The rancid smell of the monster's hidden rot mixed with half-decayed seaweed fills his nostrils. Looking down, disgusted, his stomach contents are expelled with vigour, finishing off this revolting masterpiece.

The young cadets above him are no longer screaming. They are no longer moaning. They are dead and the only sound from above is the alien ranting of a monster — a monster that he must now kill.

"What am I doing?" he whispers. Blood drips down his arm and, in his mouth, he can taste more. "Sorry Talon."

Driving the blades of his boots into the cliff face, freeing his hands, he changes his air cannon into a grappling hook. Knowing the leader to be directly above him, Tommy fires the hook over to the left of the clifftop. The leader, up above, can be heard issuing orders to his remaining followers.

"Send word to the Dehas. Tell them what has happened. Tell them the ritual to the north was interrupted. Go! I will personally take care of this human flea."

The cloaked monsters hesitate briefly. One of the beasts clicks its mandibles together in a short series. The others look at him and then look at the woods. The clicks could be roughly translated as: *I'm sure the woods just smiled at me.*

There is a swooshing sound, and a blur behind them. The Barrenites freeze, their mandibles clicking frantically. Then — with blood gushing from their neck stumps almost as high again as their bodies — their heads topple off and roll towards their leader. The leader stumbles backwards. Laughter floats down from high in the trees. A deep laughter paired with a grinding sound — like bone sliding on bone. From near the top of a pine tree, red eyes burn — like twin hell pits of death.

Tommy reaches the summit, scrambles over the top, and freezes. His eyes take in an unsettling diorama: limbs are scattered everywhere, cadets are twitching in the final stages of blood loss, and bodies of all types are woven together in a grotesque tapestry of meat. Unidentifiable organs are laid bare for the hungry birds to peck at — it is a veritable banquet for scavengers. The metallic reek of blood taints the air near the bodies.

The leader of the Barrenites is standing in a nest of guts, limbs and heads. He turns his malformed head from the forest towards Tommy. At that moment, Tommy fires the grappling hook at the creature's midsection — not having time to change the projectile into something more suitable. The leader simply sidesteps and charges. Moving in unnaturally large bounds, he is upon Tommy in an instant, hitting Tommy in the ribs. Tommy is blasted backwards with the awesome power of the impact, regaining his balance barely before plummeting off the edge of the cliff. Lightning fast, the Leader follows up with a destructive blow to the face. Tommy's nose explodes. Blood flows. Tommy's vision blurs with tears and he fights to keep conscious. The monster's hand grips Tommy's neck and — extending his arm, as if Tommy were as light as a doll — it holds him out over the hundred-foot drop.

"Who are you? Who sent you? How many are in the trees?" The Barrenite asks, spittle flying.

Tommy is trying to retract the golden cable of the grappling hooks, but his CerebroTech does not react well to the confused thoughts of those who are concussed. So, as Tommy struggles ineffectually to loosen the vice-like grip from around his neck, the gold cable and the silver grappling hooks spasm around, far below him, like an eel pegged to the shore.

"Who sent you?" the thing repeats. "Who's in the trees?"

Hearing no response from Tommy, the creature's round, onyx eyes search the gory clearing. Mouldy heaps of bones — easily mistaken for grass mounds — mark the edge of the sacrificial clearing. The old dead fence in the new, silent witnesses to the recent, if brief, suffering. The leader's eyes could not see into the dark, evergreen barrier of the firs. His eyes narrow, never leaving the treeline, and he tightens his grip on Tommy's neck. Tommy's eyes bulge, his tongue lolls and he starts to thrash about.

"Ah, Ah, Ahh," says a voice from the evergreens. "Leave him be, Reznor."

"What is the meaning of this attack? You have invaded Barrenite territory! You have broken the oath!" Reznor spits.

"Broken the oath? I wrote that oath, Reznor, as you well know. Now let Astilla go — or die like the rest. I have no desire to end you, but I know who you are and the horrors of which you are capable. I command you, as one of the seven ancients, let the human go!"

Talon drops from the tree and lands on a pile of mossy skulls. He selects one and walks towards Reznor, stroking the skull with the blade of his index finger as he walks — green mould is cleared with each swipe, revealing the shining, white bone beneath.

"The Horned One? The Lost Dehas? *Secretas?*" Reznor says with surprise.

"Really? Only three of my titles? Have you not read the chapters of the sacred book? I'm sure I have more, yes?" says Talon. His smile is very wide now, bone-plates grinding back and forth.

"The Lost Secret, Spinning Blade, Forest Demon," Reznor says, looking from Tommy to the approaching Talon.

"Stay calm, Astilla," Talon says to Tommy. "Stay still and try to control all that powerful magic." He turns his attention back to the Barrenite. "He could destroy this entire island with his magic, Reznor. Let him go."

Reznor's jet eyes narrow at Talon and then his grip on Tommy's throat loosens slightly. Eyes like stab wounds flick down to look at the glowing device attached to the human.

Reznor's grasp tightens again. Comprehension of this level of technology is beyond his intellect. Tommy starts to lose consciousness and he weakly claws at the monster's arm.

"Reznor, what other names of mine do you know?" whispers Talon as he rolls the skull over to Reznor's feet, trying to distract the Barrenite.

"You killed my clan!" Reznor screams as he savagely shakes Tommy, blood spatters from Tommy's mangled nose.

"Evil," Tommy manages to croak.

"Evil?" Reznor repeats incredulously, pulling Tommy's face close to his own.

"I've devoured many innocent lives, Reznor," says Talon. "So have you. But we were deceived. Deceived, Reznor! These are children, not food. Not mindless animals. They are not like us, but they are not our enemy. We have been wronged. Tricked by evil ones. We have been brainwashed into unspeakable acts of violence and debauchery — but there is another path. Please, release Astilla. He is my kin. He's important to me."

"These flesh sacks are responsible for the deaths of all our ancestors! How can you turn on your own kind for these pathetic, these worthless ...? These creatures are nothing more than meat for the table! This is a declaration of war, Secretas, you pathetic traitor! I promise you a war that will make up for the last ninety years of peace. I promise that the heads of your clan will burst on rocks — as mine have this day — and this monstrosity will be first!"

Reznor spits in Tommy's face, blinding his eyes with green phlegm, before dropping him off the cliff.

Before he falls two feet, Talon's arm grabs his chest. Reznor backs away in surprise before lunging for the pair. Talon throws a spluttering Tommy on to the blood-soaked grass, near a dead cadet, then he smiles his terrible, serrated, plate-bone smile.

Talon fans his finger-blades out, facing Reznor. The Barrenite lets out a war cry and charges in, swinging wildly at Talon, desperately trying to land a blow. Talon laughs and wheels around the wild, cloaked figure, dodging rapid blows with ease.

"Seems to me, Reznor, all this peace has made you forget how to fight," says Talon, as he shoves Reznor from one side to the another — passing Reznor to himself, then back again. Reznor's rage intensifies but it is an impotent rage, like shouting into a storm.

"Seems like one of those dreams when, no matter how hard you try, you just can't land a blow," chuckles Talon, dodging more of Reznor's roundhouses.

Reznor realises that suddenly he is just swinging wild blows at nothing. Looking around, he sees Talon standing several metres away, near a mound of skulls, spinning skulls on his fingers and smiling his saw-boned smile.

Tommy holds his neck, still struggling for breath, watching the crazy, one-sided fight. At one point he is convinced that Talon turned and winked at him, mid-fight. Talon's ridicule of Reznor is complete.

Talon thinks that by showing Reznor how outmatched he truly is he can convince the Barrenite to stop fighting and escort him back to the Barrenite leaders so he can personally explain what has happened. Unfortunately, Reznor has other ideas. Being a talker, but not a thinker, he says something stupid. This seals his fate.

"You and your whore's child are food for the Dehas," Reznor screams.

Talon's smile slowly fades under dark lips. His head tilts slightly and he stalks up to where the Barrenite stands panting. Reznor looks deep into the burning eyes of a demon: red eyes with something ancient and unspeakable swirling inside them. For the first time in his long life Reznor is honestly scared by what he sees.

He swings for Talon's face with a powerful right hook, trying to punch his fear away. Talon lets the creature hit him. Barely rocking Talon's head back, Reznor's fist is impaled on Talon's cheek spikes. Whipping a lethal finger blade up, Talon severs Reznor's right hand at the wrist. Screaming — his fist still affixed to Talon's face — the Barrenite backs away, trying to stem the spray of arterial blood which is quickly covering both monsters.

Talon explodes into motion, twisting like a cyclone. His vicious elbow blades blur and — with the swift accuracy of a katana wielded by a samurai sword master — slice the top off Reznor's skull, like the top of an egg. Another revolution of Talon's fatal death spin takes Reznor's eyes and nose. Yet another, removes his insulting mouth and jaw.

Reznor sways, his death arriving too fast for him to register. His hand still clasping the stump of his wrist, the Barrenite stumbles blindly toward the cliff edge. A fountain of blood almost six feet high marks the loss of Reznor's head. An almost nonchalant spinning back kick from Talon sends Reznor's decapitated body over the cliff-top edge — to join his former congregation on the rocks below.

Talon still looks fierce, glaring after the Barrenite's plunging corpse. He stands on the cliff edge, taking deep breaths — a blood-covered devil. He spits off the cliff.

"You will never speak of her again," Talon says. He walks slowly over to Tommy and lifts him gently from the floor. "I told you to stay a mile from the shore. Your stupidity nearly cost you your life, and the peace between my people and the Barrenites. What the hell were you thinking?"

"I'm sorry," says Tommy, still struggling to breathe. "I couldn't watch them die, Talon. I — I wanted to help them. Look at what they have done!"

Tommy and Talon stare over the field of massacre.

"This happens. We will help them — those we can, anyway. Check them, Astilla," says Talon. His mind far from here: in another time; another place.

Tommy moves from one body to another with little hope — he knows that he is too late. There is no way of telling how many people have died on this lonely cliffside. The large, moss-covered bone piles around the outside of the clearing are an indication of just how long this evil has been happening.

Tommy collapses to his knees amidst the carnage.

"They're dead, all of them," Tommy says. "I thought the Believers were cruel, but — what's the point in all this?" Tears fill Tommy's eyes and his shoulder aches. He walks past corpses — trying his best not to stand on, or in, them — and stops next to Talon. Together at the cliff edge they stare out over the white horse waves of the ocean.

"You were following me ...Why?" Tommy asks.

"It's beautiful here." Talon takes in deep draughts of sea air and smiles at the waves rising and falling in the sunlight.

Tommy tries to see the same beauty, but all he sees is the sun-drenched waves as sores on a bloated green-blue corpse. Tommy thinks the sea today is torturous — a cold, wet charnel house for the dead: a crypt for the recently deceased.

"You're part of the northern coastal clan. We are family, me and you. We protect our own," says Talon.

"You watched them kill the others. You could have stopped this at any time," says Tommy.

"Don't. Don't do that, Astilla! These young cadets were dead as soon as they stepped foot out of the Drumcroon facility. There's nothing I can do for such numbers. It is your father that damned them to their fate. If they hadn't died here, it would have been ten miles from here. Or twenty. In any direction. They are not equipped to survive in this place. This place belongs to those who live beneath."

"It's not my father's fault, Talon," Tommy says. "It's the Believers that control the courts, and the courts that banish these people." Tommy feels unexpectedly protective about his father. He is not sure why. Perhaps only family can insult family.

"You're talking as though he has no choice, as though these Believers control his very mind," says Talon.

"Well, no, they don't control him. But they do have a very large say in what he can do. I don't think this is the fault of just one man. And even if it is, I doubt that man is my father."

"Tommy, I have seen scores of people running this Drumcroon facility in my life. They dispatch these people out to the Barrens with no real preparation for what's actually out here. Even for my clans, there are no safe places on this land beyond our boundaries. Boundaries that many hundreds died to establish. I lost many, many friends. We prefer to shelter in the caves than risk being attacked by the Barrenites. What chance do strangers have in this land? They do not know the boundaries. They do not know how to kill. They know nothing."

"Why is it safer hiding in a cliff?" Tommy asks, trying to examine Talon's viewpoint. "You could easily get raided by Barrenites in boats. Or they could climb down the cliffs with ropes from the top. This makes no sense to me!"

"You have no idea what has happened here, Tommy. This is a place for sacrificial offerings to the Barrenite's sea god. Barrenites are terrified by the sea. They visit the shore only in small numbers and only to perform sacrifices. We rarely see them, and so are able to raise our families, and live peacefully. However, if other Barrenites find out about what happened on this clifftop, then this will be considered a contravention of our peace treaty — an act of war — and we may suffer retaliations. I'm only afraid for Daria and my clan, now. It is too much for me to try and alter the ways of the Barrenites. They are lost to ancient beliefs, things that I choose to forget."

Tommy does not see her move, but he hears a woman's weak voice. Talon watches him snake through the bodies to the source of the noise.

"This one's alive!"

Talon comes over to help the young woman. Her face is obscured by her blood-soaked hair. Tommy checks her injuries. She has a very deep cut to the head and many other wounds, just visible through the ravaged cadet uniform.

"We need to stop the bleeding!" Tommy says as he finds the worst injury: a ruined left hand, missing three fingers and part of the palm, which has clearly been bitten away. Tommy points his joining tool higher up the girl's arm, and a golden cable springs out and wraps around it. The golden tourniquet tightens and detaches from the device.

"Ok, what will it do? What happens now?" says Talon, waiting for the cables to do something interesting.

Tommy brushes the long, blood-drenched hair away from the girl's face and is taken aback.

I know you, thinks Tommy. He shakes off the thought, there are more pressing concerns.

The girl's eyes are open, but her stare is vacant. Her pale, bloodied face is frozen with fear — the horrors she recently witnessed locking her in this state. Tommy only glimpsed an image of her companions being killed but this poor soul had experienced the militarised *Hell Lights* version of events. Tommy feels sick.

"Can you fix her with this?" Talon asks, tapping one of his dark blades on Tommy's adapted arm.

"I need things. The Barrenites, do they have venom in their bites? She's dying, and I can't help her, Talon. I need more equipment. I need to treat her for the venom, but I don't recognise the symptoms."

"Some Barrenites, from the line of Funerela, have poison sacs in their mouths, but I couldn't tell you what it does to men, though," says Talon.

Tommy's MechVision is busy analysing the girl's biometric data as Tommy places the joining tools onto the girl's wounds. The findings suggest an unrecognised poison. No treatment suggestions scroll down, just her prognosis: death. A small hourglass icon appears in Tommy's MechVision and a countdown starts.

Tommy tells Talon.

"Well, let's not waste any more time, Astilla!" Talon throws the injured young lady over one shoulder and springs into the high branches of a pine tree twenty feet away.

"Follow the shore to the sea towers," Talon shouts back. "I will meet you there at sundown. We will be in the middle tower. You should make it in time if you start sailing now, and Slash is as fast as Rhombus keeps saying it is. Remember: keep to the sea, one mile from the coast."

Tommy waits as Talon vanishes. He strains to follow the sound of his friend's progress through the trees for a while, still in pain from his many injuries. He keeps focused on his friend disappearing until all he hears is a faint rustle of branches in the wind. He looks over the scene of the slaughter one last time. Tommy makes a promise to the souls that he failed to save this day. The mass grave surrounding him is witness to this promise, and the dead never forget.

"I will do anything in my power to rid this land of this evil."

Tommy uses his grappling hook to descend the cliff to the beach. The broken bodies of the monsters lie amidst the rocks and the stinking seaweed. Their bulging eyes and gaping mouths are frozen by death, their limbs are arrayed randomly, some in unnatural positions.

He stares and cannot control his disgust for the Barrenites.

The way they are in death, he thinks, *is a mirror of what they were in life: twisted, disgusting abominations that poison everything that is natural and pure.*

CHAPTER SEVEN
Lost in Darkness

The day the child realizes that all adults are imperfect, he becomes an adolescent; the day he forgives them, he becomes an adult; the day he forgives himself, he becomes wise.
-ALDEN NOWLAN-

7

Tommy wades through the shallow water and boards his catamaran.

Aboard the boat, Tommy sits and tentatively pokes at his broken nose.

Using sea water, he tries to clean away the dried blood as best he can.

He feels around the bone, it does not seem like a bad break — but

then, he is no medic.

Putting his fingers either side of his nose, he thinks *Fuck it!* and slowly pulls his nasal-cartilage back into alignment. The pain is sharp and fresh blood gushes immediately. He washes the rest of the blood away, and from his flask takes a long drink of water. Sailing away from the horror of the cliff, he studies the coastline, dotted with coves and inlets. The hidden bays sparkle in the sunlight, their picturesque mystique an illusion covering the harsh reality. The lie is not fooling Tommy. Not now. He sails further from the shore, from the temptation of exploration. The slaughter on the cliff haunts him still, poisoning everything he thought would be magical about this adventure. He seems mired by uncertainty, and paranoid questions fill his head. *How many of those beaches hide mass graves? How many innocent lives were lost? How much blood spilled?* With no answers forthcoming, the questions only multiply. He sails on, imagining alien eyes watching him from the shore. *Paranoia keeps you safe*, thinks Tommy.

On the calm sea the nautical miles fly by and, as the daylight fades, a small impact on the port side of Slash draws his attention. He scans the water and catches a fleeting glimpse of a shadow, keeping pace with Slash and disappearing under the boat. He thinks it could be a shark or a dolphin, so he rushes to the other side to check. Peering over the edge, he is wetly slapped in his face by something. Face reddening, and not just from the blow, Tommy falls back into the catamaran.

He did not see a tail coming out of the water, nor going back in, but guesses it must have been a shark. He laughs at his fortune — it could have bitten his head off! More cautiously this time, he returns to the side of the boat and peers beneath the racing waves. He sees nothing. Still smiling, he returns to the basics of sailing Slash.

The sky's subtle tonal changes are more appealing to Tommy as the sun sets in the west. His imagination keeps him company. The patterns in the sky are the slashes of a fire-sword carving through the pink flesh of a heavenly Titan's throat. The colours originate from an apocalyptic volcanic explosion, magma exposed, leaving fiery trails in the sky. The ever-changing sunset was a theatrical performance, placed there by the gods, to entertain Tommy on his adventure, speaking a thousand tales of ancient and forgotten mysteries.

Soon, just ahead, he could make out the jutting fingers of the towers described by Talon. Black, at first — silhouetted against the blood red sky — they grow, and their details appear rapidly. The most magnificent sunset Tommy has ever seen is about to end as he makes his final approach to the sea towers. The first three towers have light emanating from high up.

As he approaches, a sudden scream rends the dusk air. Intense fear grips him as the scream dies abruptly, halted by something, or someone. Tommy's mind pulses with frightened, barely logical ideas and scenarios. *They must not have made it. The Barrenites must have swarmed Talon, tearing him apart, dying in vast numbers.* His stomach churns as he approaches the towers. He ties his boat to the side of an old jetty and stares up a rickety, old rope ladder. At the top of this poor excuse for a ladder was a hole in the tower that flickered with firelight.

CHAPTER EIGHT
Old Idra

The only thing necessary for the triumph of evil is for good men to do nothing

-EDMUND BURKE-

8

Tommy clambers up the swaying and creaking rope ladder. Talon greets him with his frightful smile and slaps Tommy's aching back, knocking the air from his lungs, winding him. He is almost surprised at how relieved he is to see his unusual devil-faced friend alive and well.

"Welcome to Idra's tower, Astilla. You made decent time." Talon moves beside the welcoming fireplace and Tommy looks at Idra's home.

The large cave atop the plateau is a treasure trove of ancient and macabre artefacts.

Furniture is placed around the large, well-lit cavern, made from driftwood and bones — *Animal bones*, Tommy thinks; although his paranoia instantly wonders if there are not some human remains mixed in. Next, Tommy's attention is drawn to the ceiling — it is a collage of human skulls. He takes several steps backwards in shock. On the walls, the skeletons of various sea creatures are strung between skulls which are sunk into the rock, pearls blinking reflected fire from darkly shadowed sockets. A knot-work rope motif of purples, greens, and browns spread out, weblike, weaving amongst the furniture and the skeletons. Skull lanterns light the darkest areas furthest from the fire. The dancing shadows cast from these ghoulish lanterns enchants the ceiling with a chiaroscuro movement of its own. A theatrical performance of light and texture, mighty with its majesty: a sparkling, writhing universe of Death.

The focal point of the room is a huge hearth, built using the fossilised ribcage of a huge prehistoric beast, into the centre of the cavern's back wall. The fire crackles, logs spitting embers from their andiron embrace. In front of the elaborate hearth, on a deeply furred rug, lying completely naked, is the injured cadet. Bent over her pale form is a fur-covered old crone, stooped and withered with time.

Talon sits on an elaborate throne to the right of the fire — in this light, his rune-covered skin looks even more fascinating. The throne is made from the jaws of a huge sea creature somewhat like a great white shark. With the addition of furs, leather and wood, the forbidding jaw-seat seems almost comfortable.

Tommy nervously approaches the trio.

His eyes are slowly drawn to the form of the cadet lying in front of the fire. Her pale white skin contrasts with the bulbous blue leaches which are gorging on the injured woman's yellowing wounds. He watches, sickened, as their slick, shiny bodies slowly pulsate and swell with purloined blood.

"Are *they* helping her?" Inquires Tommy, his lip curling back in disgust.

"They're removing the poison," creaks the old woman. She looks at Tommy and says,

"They're also tea." She un-attaches — with an audible pop — one of the fat, blood-filled leaches and throws it into a pot bubbling on the hearth.

"No! Really?" asks Tommy as he looks towards Talon for reassurance.

Talon merely licks his lips. His tongue — Tommy now notices that it is bifurcated like a snake's tongue — licking top and bottom lips simultaneously.

"What the hell! ... Your tongue! ...It's not tea. Not, really? ... Is it?" rants Tommy.

Idra smiles now and laughs, a short, gravelly cough. Perhaps at Tommy's disgust, perhaps at his naivety. She pulls the remaining blood-filled leeches off the girl and casts them into the pot. She wraps thick furs around the young cadet and sits in a chair facing Talon. The hag gestures Tommy to pull up a seat by the fire. Talon pokes the fire, throws on more wood and the flames start to roar higher in the hearth. Tommy notices a natural-looking vent that takes the fire-smoke far up and out the top of the tower. The cadet stirs in her unconsciousness, wrapped up like a furry chrysalis — oblivious to her strange surroundings.

"Get rid of that for me will you, Secretas," says Idra, wafting a hand towards the steaming stew pot. Tommy remembers that the Barrenite at the clifftop, Reznor, also used that same name for Talon. Talon catches Tommy's confused look and just smiles, winking as he taps the side of his nose with a long index finger-blade. Tommy shrugs. He realises that he does not care. Maybe if they all existed in a different time — a time when he was not so tired, irritable, and hungry — maybe then he would question this odd name, *Secretas*.

Talon goes to the cave mouth, looks to see that there is no one coming to visit the old lady, then hurls the boiling filth down into the sea. Tommy watches as the crone settles into her carved wood, patchwork, pelt-covered chair. He is a little curious as to what kind of strange life Idra must have had to end up in a high tower, living in a death-encrusted cave. She grabs at a long wooden pipe that is on a nearby stool and clutches at a long cane that is also nearby. Popping the pipe in her mouth, Idra jabs the cane into the fire causing glowing red embers to spark and pop. Cane still in the fire, she winks at Tommy and then has a small coughing fit, before returning her attention to the cane. Pulling the stick quickly through her hands, she uses the small flame on its end to light her pipe. Taking deep drags from the pipe, Idra sinks into the furs of her chair and a smile grows on her wrinkled face. The smoke has a sweet scent to it that Tommy finds calming. Once the old lady is suitably settled, she addresses Tommy.

"I'm Idra. You must be this magical boy that Talon has told me all about." The old lady expels smoke and stares at Tommy's strange arm. She tries hard to fight off another coughing fit — but fails.

"Would you prefer it if I took the joining tools off?" Tommy asks, glancing at Talon.

"Leave them on, take them off, I have no problem," says Idra as she puffs on her pipe — her small eyes gleaming like the pearl-eyes of the skulls watching from the walls and ceiling.

"I prefer to keep them on," Tommy says. He looks away from Idra's piercing eyes, unable, or unwilling, to hold them for long. Idra's was a haunting, searching stare — studying Tommy, troubling him. It was a familiar stare, too. He has felt a similar feeling many times before when Pandeminia, the clan's name-giver, had looked into his eyes. It is a strange pressure in his skull, as if his mind is suddenly crowded. The way Idra stared deep into his eyes was more than uncomfortable. She is, clearly, a more powerful telepath than Pandeminia. Magnet-like, Tommy's gaze is drawn back to those gimlet eyes, boring into him, and Idra accesses Tommy's memories. Memories of his life in the Drumcroon facility, of his Mother and Father, of the pregnant woman being shot, of his feelings of solitude, hopelessness, and despair. Tommy's mind bounces from one different memory to another, Tommy looking on, a passenger in his own vehicle of recall. His memories are like images in an NTB pod being shuffled through by Idra as she searches out who he is. She arrives at a memory that Tommy no longer cares to remember, one that he had hidden, and his unconscious strains to pull her away from this cold dark place. Sensing his anguish, she relents and instead looks upon a happier memory.

In the memory, Tommy is finishing the design for the Eternal Power Clamp. Beaming, singing to himself with pure elation, he feels light and happy, like anything is possible in this mood. Taking Tommy to this relaxing feeling, Idra's mind-invasion continues. His memories swirl, he feels Idra flicking through memory after memory, skim-reading his past. Idra is now looking at memories in which Tommy loses his temper. A screaming voice arises in him, wanting her to stop — but, ignoring it, she steps inside a locked room in his mind.

Idra watches Tommy at the Diamond Lights School for the Gifted, as the teacher instructs him to hand over whatever it is he has behind his back. Tommy grimaces, bringing his arm into view. His right arm is bleeding badly, in places, and there are lumps of metal protruding here and there.

"What is this Tommy? What have you done to yourself?" the teacher in his memory says.

"It's not finished. I think something went wrong. I need more time," Tommy says through tears, his anger spilling out. In the memory, the other kids look at Tommy and one of them smirks at him, mockingly chanting Tommy's name, not-so-quietly under his breath. Tommy hears this, and anger raises its head, mixes with shame and frustration of his discovery and his arm starts to glow.

"Tommy? What's happening?" The teacher now has both palms held up placatingly to Tommy — trying to control the strange situation that is unfolding. His brain is too Optimal, he has no idea what is happening.

"Get away from me!" Tommy shouts, as the teacher approaches.

Tommy's arm is shining a violet light and bulging outwards in green and yellow patches. Blue and green vein-like tentacles flash under his skin, kaleidoscopic colours strobe. His flesh separates in places to reveal cables and veins, lights sparking and fizzing like a frayed power cable in the rain.

"I got the mixture wrong; I think. I should have known better. Ahhhh!" In pain now, Tommy pushes a chair away, wildly looking around, scanning the room for an exit. In his panic, he forgets where he is, and the experimental implants dig deeper into his flesh. Tommy crumples over, doubles up, tucking his mutilated arm protectively into his stomach. Using only the strength of his mind he tries to reduce the pain, tries to stay conscious. His other hand clenches into a whitening fist as the pain steadily increases.

Tommy's teacher cautiously approaches.

"There, there, Tommy. Everything's going to be okay. You must have just hurt yourself by accident? Isn't that right? Tommy?" The teacher places his hand on Tommy's back and rubs it up and down, soothingly. There is an explosion of violet energy and the teacher flies backwards, striking the far wall of the classroom with a sickeningly wet thud. The other children stare from the slumped body of the teacher to Tommy.

"Stop looking!" Tommy's nine-year-old self screams.

Somewhere inside his head he hears Idra chuckle, and then another hidden memory reveals itself. And another. And another. They play like movies in his memory's eye, and helpless, he watches them.

The telepathic connection between Tommy and Idra suddenly broken, Tommy's consciousness snaps back to the warmth of Idra's cave.

Tommy holds his head for a second or two, a deep burning inside his brain. Idra stares into the fire, puffing her pipe, a strange smirk on her face as she chews the stem of her bone pipe.

"What the hell was that! Stay out of my head, old lady!" Tommy shouts with one hand clamped over his right eye, trying — and failing — to hold the hot pain at bay.

Idra sees Talon moving behind Tommy, but speaks quietly, softly to the shocked young man, "Your memories are re-filing themselves. You'll feel better in a minute or two. I find that trying to get to know someone with just words is too — um, how should I say — boring ... noooo, not boring ... longwinded. Yessss, long-winded. And, when you are my age, you realise that time is a great treasure. A great treasure that others try to steal from you."

Talon looks over at Idra, smiles and starts to riffle through jars of spices, shaking his head, as if he has heard this speech a thousand times before.

"I'm too old to waste my lung power on asking things over and over again," she continues, "hearing words that don't come close to whom one is, what one does, or if one is maybe more than one."

"I want my head to shut up," Tommy says, blinking frantically to shake off the last bit of the old woman's invasiveness. "I just want peace."

"Just want peace? *Just?*" says Idra.

"Yeah, what's wrong with that?" Tommy asks.

"My dear, sweet boy — you've no idea, do you? It's not possible for you to be at peace." Idra pokes at her pipe's bowl disinterestedly.

Tommy looks shocked. He waits for elaboration. He needs her to explain herself and so he waits.

Old Idra taps out her pipe, blissfully ignorant of Tommy's impatience, and refills it from a pouch hung around her neck. She repeats the stick trick to light the bowl. Tommy's frustration with the Old Lady's reticence reaches critical mass.

"Why?" Tommy explodes, rubbing his now throbbing head with both hands.

Idra takes a few deep tokes, reclines in her chair, and stares at the intricate skull-ceiling, a cloud of pipe smoke pooling above, her eyes narrowing lost in thought, or memories, or herbs.

"Why...? Why...? Why...?" Idra repeats — each word punctuated by a little smoke ring which drifts up to the smoke sea gathering above, dotted with islands of skull. "You can't be at peace," she says, "because only children know true peace. And you've never been a child."

"What?" spits Tommy.

"It's also because you're an ... angry ... little ... shit!" Says Idra — sending three more expanding rings to disappear into the smoky sea of skulls. She claps her hands together and falls over, laughing hysterically and starting another coughing fit.

Looking over to Talon for support, Tommy notices his friend trying hard not to laugh himself, still hunched over jars of herbs.

Rubbing his head further, this time with frustration, Tommy takes an angry swig from his flask.

'I was never a child?' Tommy repeats, mostly to himself, trying to decipher the message. His sips the cool water from the flask trying to douse the fiery embers of his anger.

"You were never a child doing childlike things. And, because of that, you never really learned to have fun. Fun was, and still is, alien to you. Fun is something you've seen others do. So, when you say you just want to be at peace, you're really saying, 'Just leave me alone. I don't know what I want and —'" here she pauses dramatically — "'and ...*and* ...I'm an angry little shit!'" Idra bursts into coughing hysterics once more. Dropping a jar of herbs, Talon also erupts into hearty laughter which makes even the confused Tommy laugh, because Talon's laugh did that to people.

"Okay, okay," Tommy says, "but what should I do about it? What do I need to change to find peace?"

"Oh dear, no. No, child. You're worse than I thought. No, you carry on about your business, as usual. You don't want to change on my account, or anyone else's either. There are many ways in which people organise what's important in their life. As an example, some people never think about how to live, they just live. They take life for what it is — a random arrangement of brief, fleeting moments. They are happy in this chaos. Happy not to try and make order out of the unordered. There are some who are naturally happy, no matter what the world brings, and there are others, like yourself, who are not. For whatever reason, those like you believe that they should organise and plan everything — even happiness. 'Let's put aside some time in the calendar,' they say, 'in — oh, I don't know — late June, late June early July; then fun shall happen!'" Idra smiled kindly at the gaping Tommy.

"That does seem a bit like me," says Tommy with a rueful smile.

"You're also hungry and tired —" Idra says "— but then, I don't have to be a mind reader to know that. Listen, there is nothing wrong with being the way you are, but, maybe, take a moment sometimes to stop and *just* — I know you like that word! — enjoy life. You can't organise everything; you can't predict everything. Trying to do so will only strain you and make you ill."

"What if I can't stop?" Tommy asks.

"Find someone who will make you stop, or else find someone who won't care — but never pretend to be that which you are not. It would be a shame for a budding flower to die in the shadows. Carry on down your path, Tommy. Who knows, maybe you will be the one who figures this whole thing out? And, if you do, you'll know exactly what is coming next. How much fun would that be? To become a God, imagine that — because that's what the mastery of imagination and creation does. There are no surprises for those that author reality," says Idra, tapping her pipe out again.

It is that simple to Idra. She sees the way people are and how they can be. She neither changes nor judges them; she merely tells them how it is. To some, this revelation feels like she has cooked a part of their brain; to others, it feels like a dip in iced water, and to yet others, the revelation is greeted with a sense of calm that falls upon them. Old Idra has a fantastic gift.

"Also, before we eat," she continues, "the dream you had of Daria and Talon scared you, yes? Other people organise this darkness that is the human soul, you see. None more so than those that cause the atrocities, the ancient wars, the brainwashing needed to believe that we, as humans, are somehow indebted to a higher force. Hmm?" Tommy stares at Idra, uncomprehending.

Talon has been bustling around with bowls and eating implements but stops as he overhears this portion of the conversation. "Tantum relligio potuit suadere malorum," Talon adds gravely.

Idra smiles at Tommy's increased confusion. "So great are the evils Religion had encouraged," she translates.

"In the ancient world, before the flood, an ancient race called the Carthaginians sacrificed some of their children to appease a god called Saturn — the planet we know was named for this god. Those picked, who had no children, bought some. The parents had to attend the sacrificial service and look happy, content. It is a strange notion to seek divine goodness amidst such cruelty. Another ancient race, the Spartans, flogged young boys — sometimes to death — to appease Diana, their goddess of The Hunt. It's a savage humour to please the architect by destroying what she (or he) has built; to ward off the judgement of the guilty by punishing the pure. There are many such examples throughout the ancient history of humans. Different gods and different people but the same, sad tragedy plays out each, and every, time. All the known religions produced, and still produce, bloodshed and anguish. Look at the Believers, Tommy. Look and let these dreams not shock you anymore, child. Humans are flawed and fooled easily by fear of the infinite and the despair of nothingness. Imagination is what both frees us and binds us, the portion different in each instance. You're different, Astilla. I think that, in the end, you'll be okay."

Idra and Tommy both smile at one another whilst Talon arranges containers of powdered goods before himself and Tommy.

"Food preparation time," says Talon, ruffling Tommy's hair. Tommy wanted to quiz Talon on what had just happened to his brain, but he felt too tired to start an in-depth conversation about Old Idra's talents.

"That's good. I'm *so* hungry. Actually, Talon, where is the food?" asks Tommy.

"I GOT FOOD!" thunders a voice so loud that it makes Talon and Tommy jump a little. Old Idra does not flinch. *Perhaps her hearing is going*, thinks Tommy, a little maliciously.

"Oh no, not *that* glutton! Who dragged him in here?" huffs the old woman.

Talon flicks one of his huge blade fingers out towards Tommy.

"Astilla's fault!" says Talon.

"THANKWELL'S BROUGHT FOOD!" says the dripping Thankwell, beaming a shark-like grin.

Thankwell and Talon prepare the delicious-looking bounty of barracuda and mussels that Thankwell has foraged from his beloved aquatic kingdom.

"Have you been following me, Thankwell? How?" Tommy asks.

"Under," grunts Thankwell, banging water from one of his ears. Tommy knows that Thankwell hates using more words than necessary, but he chooses to pry anyway.

"Underwater... yes?" Tommy says slowly, and nodding his head, as if to will a response from the huge man's pallid face.

Thankwell just nods, strands of seaweed swinging from his head, and places the backs of his hands together. He looks at Tommy's confused face searching it for understanding.

"Under!" he repeats and shakes his joined hands at Tommy. Tommy smiles at the bland huge head of Thankwell and looks over to Talon for a little help. Clearly the short time he spent learning to sail with the giant man did not help his understanding as much as Tommy thought it had.

"Down, down deep and under," Thankwell said again, banging the other side of his head — water spraying from the opposite ear.

His head must be hollow! Tommy thinks with exasperation. Frustrated with Thankwell's non-answers, Tommy slows down his speech further. "How... Did... You... Get.... Here... So... Fast?"

Thankwell stares at Tommy — his eyes narrow, his large muscular jaw tightens. Idra cackles and Talon wisely decides to intercede.

"Thankwell likes to dive, Tommy. He has a rope tied to the bottom of every boat back at our bay. He just grabs a rope, stays underwater, and hitches a lift with whichever boat he fancies. Isn't that right, old friend?" Talon says.

"He always brings weird and wonderful things back here," says Idra, ambling over to the man-mountain and reaching up on tiptoes to stroke a wet cheek.

"Give it rest, mom," says a now bashful Thankwell.

Tommy smirks a little at a giant man having his cheek pinched by an old woman. Tommy found the scene ridiculous. *This giant man actually had a mother? Was he adopted? And* she *made* him *bashful?*

Thankwell catches a glimpse of Tommy's smirk. In irritation, he launches a shield he has on his back and the disk spins towards Tommy's head. Before the shield hits Tommy in the face, Talon plucks the projectile from the air with his blade fingers, chuckling at his oversensitive friend. This uncomfortable situation is the sort that Talon loves to see — he is, however, quite surprised that Tommy did not flinch.

Tommy frowns at Thankwell and turns his attention to the young Cadet who is now making strange noises.

"Will she be okay, Idra?" Tommy asks, as the charge in his modified arm cools — no one else seemed to have noticed it had charged automatically during Thankwell's attack.

"The poison is strong but, if she survives the night, she'll survive the poison," says Talon, still eyeing Thankwell.

Talon returns to the comfort of his shark throne with Thankwell's shield and places all the food onto it.

"Yes, yes," says Idra — clearly irritated by Talon answering for her. She settles, groaning, into her creaking chair. Thankwell brings Talon several jars, clipping Tommy round the back of the head with a light slap *en passant*. Tommy jumps up and returns the blow with a heavy kick to the big man's backside, but his metal blast boot barely makes an impression in the absorbent grey and white blubber covering Thankwell's rump.

Thankwell wraps himself in some large furs and then goes and ferries the jars from Talon to Tommy. "Take lids off," Thankwell says to Tommy. "Talon 'n' lids ... don't work."

"Talons do work well for gutting whales, though," Talon says, wagging a pointy index finger at Thankwell.

Ignoring the banter, Thankwell points and grunts in the direction of the space cadet, his seaweed-entangled hair still dripping on the floor.

"Yes, she can be moved, son," Idra says. "She's had enough heat — place her in a hammock for a while."

Tommy notes how delicately the giant man scoops up the fragile cadet, his shark-like maw hanging open in concentration. An unwanted thought springs into Tommy's head, *Thankwell could bite the young cadet's head off, should he want to.* Talon lowers down a long hammock with a hidden winch system and Thankwell places the young fur-wrapped girl gently into the hammock, her weight sealing her into it.

A large tree trunk table is rolled in front of the fire, replacing the empty space left by the injured cadet. While Talon pours some dark liquid into the caldron, the fire is stoked, and the cauldron is then returned to the fire. The fire is blazing high now and, as his flesh passes over the flames, pushing the caldron to the rear of the fire, Talon's tribal runes glow a deep red, with orange flecks.

Talon scoops coloured powders from the jars proffered by Thankwell, seems to measure the amounts on his bladelike fingers, and then flicks the powders over the *Fruit de Mer*.

"Seasoning makes food better," Thankwell says, drooling long lines of saliva onto the floor.

"You love your seasoning, don't you, my boy!" Idra says, moving towards her massive child.

"Yeah, love seasoning ... stop it!" The squirming lump of a man almost squeals as his mother pinches rolls of belly flab and starts shaking it around. Thankwell puts the jars of seasoning away grumbling to himself and then sits down, glowering, obviously embarrassed. Tommy looks — wide-eyed, trying not to chuckle — at Talon and Talon returns a smirking warning glance. The demonic man fills wooden goblets, using a long wooden ladle, with steaming brown liquid from the cauldron.

"You've done a more than respectable job with this bountiful feast, Thankwell. I think that I can speak for all of us here when I say —" Talon places warm beakers of hot brown liquid in each person's hand and returns to his seat in a blur of action. Holding up his long arm, grandiosely, the wooden tankard raised aloft, he finished — "Thank you, Thankwell!"

"Secretas, you know I hate it when you move fast!" Idra scolds, as she places her pipe down. "It gives me a fair headache." The old woman then raises her own arm, like a brown, knotted length of string, and nods towards Talon.

"*THANK YOU, THANKWELL!*" Roar Talon and Idra.

Thankwell is looking extremely pleased with himself and Tommy feels the whole scene is an amusing end to a very traumatic day. Sipping the drink, toasting Thankwell's foraging skills, he is amazed by the beverage. It both warms and soothes him from the inside out. It is delicious. Bizarrely, he cannot recognise the flavour.

"What is this? It's — Amazing," says Tommy, with another eager gulp.

"Idra's famous tonic," says Talon, reclining back and using a long tool to flip over the food sizzling now on Thankwell's ancient shield over the fire.

"What's it made from, Idra? It's like nothing I've ever had before. Very refreshing." Tommy necks the lot and then offers up the tankard for Talon to refill — which he does, albeit reluctantly.

"It's an ancient family recipe, Tommy. I can tell you that two of the ingredients are sarsaparilla and seaweed, but the others are a secret. Obviously, I know the recipe, my boy knows it and, if he gets around to having a family of his own, he will no doubt choose to pass the secret of the recipe down to them."

"Won't tell anyone," says Thankwell.

"Good boy, Thankwell," says Idra.

"Come now, Idra, after all that I've done for you and yours, you won't even tell good, old Talon?" Talon says with a joking seriousness, filling his cup again.

She smirks, watching him smile and drink. She is still, after all these years, fascinated by his engraved skin. It is almost as if she forgets the mystique of his magically carved runes when he is away.

"Old you are, Talon. Yes, well you win on that one — but you are yet to see the real face of age. I doubt very much if you will see your feet break apart, your spine curve and your strength fade away to almost nothing. No, not even you Talon — even after all you have done for me and mine — you'll never know the secret of Idra's Tonic. It is my secret, mine and my boy's."

Idra held out a delicate hand towards Thankwell who took it gently, holding her entire hand between his thumb and forefinger. They shared the secret and sacred smile of mother and son.

"I'll not tell, Talon!" Thankwell laughs, as Talon refills Thankwell's large tankard with the beverage.

"Well, as long as it keeps getting made, I think I can live without knowing the secret," Talon says. "It pains me, Idra. You know that. It pains me to think I will never have the recipe for this wondrous elixir," the mock defeat in Talon's voice is theatrically thick.

"Agreed," says Tommy, feeling remarkably light-headed, but content and happy. "It's too good not to have any more and, as long as the secret's safe with you two ..."

"You'll never know it," says Thankwell, staring at the grinning drunk that is Tommy Salem.

"Good, yes. Good-men, Thanks-swells," slurs Tommy as his eyes begin to shrink into mice-eyes. He reaches out and begins pawing Thankwell's large face. "Yes, yes, good boy. Good man, Thanks-swell, yes, yes," slurs Tommy.

Thankwell softly shoves him with a thick finger and Tommy falls backwards off his seat with a funny look on his face, blowing brown bubbles from between his lips and smiling inanely.

Talon smirks and turns over the sizzling fish. He will leave some food for Tommy to have in the morning — there is no chance of him waking for a good six hours, or so. Tommy was far too gone. Drunk on the strong alcohol of Idra's famous restorative tonic.

━━━━╫╲╲╫╪━━━━

Tommy awakes with a jolt, lashing out with his natural arm at the fading, tormenting visions of death and demons, and a clifftop.

Talon is loading up the fire with bundles of sticks and logs. The cave top sanctuary resonates with the loud, thunderous snores of Thankwell, and the slightly quieter snores of the elderly Idra — mother and son synchronised in their appalling noise making. Tommy's head feels like it did after first meeting with Talon — like someone has smashed him over the head with a log.

"Saturn's rings! What ...What the fuck's going on?" says Tommy.

"You had too much Tonic," Says Talon.

Tommy's head throbs: there is noise everywhere. The snores feel like cannons in his ears, the crackle of the fire is almost deafening, and even his heartbeat and breathing seem unnaturally noisy. Everything is amplified; everything is annoyingly painful. Tommy clasps his head and tries to bury himself in bed furs.

"The evil wench poisoned me with a tonic!"

"You drank it, Astilla!" laughs Talon, pouring some more tonic and handing it to him.

"What's this?" Tommy asks feebly, wondering if Talon can dial down the volume of his laughing.

"More of the same. Hair of the dog," says Talon.

"What bloody dog?"

"The dog that bit you last night, Tommy."

"Dog? What? No. What the hell? No, thanks. I'm never touching that shit again!" Tommy says looking at the hateful brown liquid and feeling nausea filling him up, his mouth watering and his stomach churning.

"If you want the pain in your head to end, you'll do well to listen," Talon says more sternly.

With considerable effort, Tommy manages to get the tonic down and keep it there. It tastes as fine as it did last night and, within a few minutes, he feels the pain in his head lessen.

"It's getting better. Well, it's less bad, anyway. Thanks, Talon," says Tommy.

"Anytime," Talon replies. "Once you have one more small draught, try to eat something. You have a little ways left to go yet on your westward journey to be safe and to live with your kind. Travelling can't be done either on an empty stomach or a full head."

"How is she?" Tommy asks, nodding towards the hammock.

"She's survived the night, so her resilience is good. It looks like we have a real fighter on our hands." Talon goes back to his shark-toothed seat beside the constantly lit fire. "It reminds me of when I found Idra," Talon says, stretching his arms above his head, the dangerous blades of his hands interlinked, his elbows cracking. Once his stretch is complete, he offers Tommy more of Idra's potion. Tommy starts to pick at his food and *sip* the potion — *Once bitten, twice shy*, Tommy thinks — as Talon considers the flames, his eyes seeing ancient memories play out in the sparkling and crackling colours of the plasma.

"Please, tell me the story," Tommy says, finding his appetite returning with a vengeance and gorging on the delicious, and well-seasoned, seafood.

"It was during the war between the coastal tribes and the Barrenites. It's a difficult time for me to think about because I was in love; and was loved in return — for what seemed like an eternity — and I felt that love would triumph. But sometimes, young Tommy, life confutes our fondest wishes. Sometimes eternity is *not* long enough, and sometimes love *is* lost."

A solitary tear traced its way down Talon's face, like a fast-moving glacier in the mountainous spikes of Talons cheeks. Tears now came easily and unwithheld and they filled the empty riverbeds of his carved runes and flowed — rivers of sorrow.

"Being around Idra always makes me think of her. Suddenly she's there — so real, so vivid in my mind — so golden and perfect — an angel from another time and place. A better time. A better place."

"We don't have to talk about it if it upsets you, Talon," Tommy says quickly.

But Talon no longer seems to be listening. He had stayed up all night, watching over the young cadet, drinking tonic the whole time, and is now lost in the long past of his ancient life, wrapped within the soothing embrace of Idra's tonic. Talon fills up yet another tankard of steaming tonic and drinks deeply, his mind flowing back into his past.

"I like to remember her. My love — my Aurum — was the last link to my life before the clan. Idra helped me to deal with who I was, who I had been, and what I could become. She's incredibly wise, Idra, wiser than I could ever be. Exceedingly rare to get true wisdom, yes? It's a myth that it comes with age, a fantasy. It really does help to know someone like her — she got me through the worst times, where all hope seemed lost. After Aurum left this world, I would walk around the island for days without rest — I had lost my true love, and with her, hope."

Tommy takes deep gulps from his patchwork flask — the one Talon had given him. He has it on a long-braided strip of leather stretching from right shoulder to left hip — it feels almost part of him, like it has always belonged to him. He looks at Talon, who is blankly staring over at the still sleeping Idra, who, in sleep, looks even older.

"What you see before you, in me, is the finished result of her ninety-six years of counselling me, through things no one should have to hear about."

"Idra's that old?" Tommy asks with surprise.

"She's not like anyone I've ever met. She surprises even me — after all my years on this planet. The thing that amazes me most is her life force. Her body has been beaten and hurt in innumerable, unimaginable ways and yet that luminescent essence that is inside her still shines through. She is not afraid to show compassion to anyone, not even to a demon. A demon whose feet she bathed and who said to him — told him — that he *could* be clean."

"She's so *old*," Tommy says in an awed and slightly tipsy whisper, as he looks to the napping elderly woman wrapped in furs.

Talon fills another tankard of the lethally alcoholic tonic. The tonic's effects on the demon seemed muted and, perhaps, they were transient — which would explain why Talon was drinking so much. Tommy is sure that he would probably be long dead if he tried to drink one-hundredth of what his strange friend had consumed.

Talon returns his attention to the flames, and in fire and fermented drink, he begins to tell his story ...

CHAPTER NINE

Talon's Trials

All human wisdom is summed up in two
words; wait and hope.

-Alexandre Dumas-

9

"**B**efore I came to this place, this reality, there were changes made to the volume of prisoners passing through the Drumcroon facility. Prisoner processing numbers increased to surpass what they called 'critical mass.' The two people in charge of the Island during this time were called Professor Aldous Matheson and Dr Caroline Brogan. They bribed senior officials of the Believers' court to send them more prisoners. At first, it seemed to many that Matheson wanted more prisoners to impress his superiors and gain credits, to have his prison being lauded as the best in all the known universe. Later, it was shown that Matheson used the prisoners to increase his sense of power. Controlling lives was intoxicating for him, and he behaved like any addict — doing anything for a fix. He also needed the prisoners for his experiments. Professor Matheson and Dr Caroline Brogan had one true shared passion — the collection and study of the mind; more specifically: dreams, memories and nightmares.

"It was Matheson who created the revolutionary 'memory plates.' But his creative genius stretched far beyond the simple parameters of technological wizardry. Matheson didn't just wish to learn what could be retrieved from deep, deep within the human mind — in the subconscious realms of dreams and nightmares — he wanted to go beyond, to the source.

"The extractions were made possible by a technique invented by an expert in neurological dream extraction, Dr Caroline Brogan. She tapped into the more ancient parts of the human brain, collectively called the limbic system, where memories are made and processed. Brogan and Matheson found they shared a love of exploring the unknown, dark portals that existed inside the consciousness of every human — portals housing shadowy figures that restlessly stirred within their limbic labyrinths. These strange portals from another world could be visited, data retrieved and then extrapolated, added to, given form — making fantasy into flesh and blood. Matheson and Brogan extracted the most twisted visions from the minds of prisoners, recreated their visions in all their delightful horror and then forced the creators to face their own personal hells.

"By this time, the population of the island was vast. It had spread out over the landmass in 'reservations' and then overspilled into the sea, where pirate communities thrived and built villages and harbours and galleons. They had created a life for themselves. A civilisation, of sorts — in the loosest of possible terms. Faced with this ever-increasing prison population, Matheson and Brogan did what any self-righteous god would do and decided upon a cull. It was flood time — and this time they chose the Noahs.

"In the learned doctors' demented opinion, this planet was being treated like a paradise. This was no prison to the people, the convicts, living free in the settlements and prospering. Matheson and Brogan both wanted more punishment. They wanted the convicts to suffer. They wanted this island to be a Hell. They wanted to throw their prisoners to ravening wolves and bears. They wanted to throw them to ... *worse* things."

Tommy could have sworn Talon's eyes flared from black to red for the briefest of moments, but he put this down to an illusion of the flickering firelight.

Tommy looks over to the sleeping Idra and Thankwell. Idra stirs slightly, but her hearing is not good, so she sleeps on. Thankwell lifts one heavy eyelid and peeks over to his mother then over to Talon and simply says 'Hush,' before returning to his dreams.

"You don't have to carry on, Talon. I can see the telling hurts," says Tommy.

"It's been so long since I spoke of these things that it'll pain me more *not* to continue."

Talon stares into the dancing flames of the fire, his dangerous hands flexing.

Tommy waits for Talon to continue his story, not wanting to put pressure on his friend, allowing him to tell his story in his own time. He cannot help but feel pity in the presence of a being who radiates so much hurt, but he knows Talon would not want his pity.

Nursing a new tankard of potion, Talon continues ...

"My kind tell ourselves an elaborate mythology. The Barrenites are the last of an ancient tribe that existed long before the tribe of humans. We tell ourselves that evil humans exterminated our ancestors and that the Guardians, led by Matheson and Brogan, defected from these evil persecutors, and joined with us to help our people survive. Matheson and Brogan told us our birth parents had given us, just seven children, to the doctors to raise and charged them to re-populate the world with our tribe. The doctors professed to be conservationists who had rebelled against their bloodthirsty species and tried to help our tribe — and this was backed up by fake pictures and memory plate footage. There is footage of our parents giving us lasting advice and I have a picture of my mother kissing me, kissing my head, and weeping over my cot. There was no way of knowing that the footage was forged. These false memories hurt me still.

"In these counterfeit memories, my parents looked much as I do. I would try to imagine what they were thinking, as they left me. I'd try to stare through the monitor at these recordings and read my mother's body language, looking for signs, for some clue as to why they left me here. Records on memory plates, parents speaking from beyond the grave — it was very convincing.

"None of us doubted Matheson and Brogan's story and they became our saviours. They named us *The Seven Dehas*, and they joked between themselves over which of us was going to be the most lethal. Seven innocent children. Strange and gifted children, but children all the same.

"Raised in the Drumcroon facility together — living in NTB rooms, programmed by Matheson and Brogan — we were a family. We lived to make the doctors happy. They were our elders, and the only parents we had ever known.

"The extensive alterations to our genomes, our abominable mutations, kept us bound to one another and placed an almost insurmountable barrier between us and humans.

"The children were four girls and three boys, including myself. The doctors bred us in those ratios for psychological reasons, and the girls were a calming influence on us boys.

Matheson and Brogan seemed to have thought of everything. Their intention was to use the seven of us as breeding stock, prize bullocks and cows. They planned to use the seven of us as a control mechanism, a *natural* check on the prisoner population. And they also intended to, somehow, keep us a secret from the Believers and the other Guardians. We were to be tools. Tools engineered to kill those who had forfeited their humanity by being condemned by the Believers at their courts. We, the seven *in-humans*, were to be used to kill Them, the plague of *sub-humans*. We were the beasts killing Christians in the Colosseum; we were the Biblical flood drowning the impure — Matheson and Brogan's Final Solution.

"We watched as these humans turned up, spilled out over the island, and went about their lives. At the time, I remember our over-riding feelings were of disgust at these pathetic creatures that infested our land.

"We were brainwashed from birth to think that we had always been here and that these humans had deceived our kind, trapped and killed our parents, and that the good doctors and the rest of the Guardians had saved us from these savages.

"When the doctors had wound us up enough, they finally unleashed the seven Dehas upon prison planet Earth. We decimated the settlements worse than biblical plagues, and the carnage was such that, in parts, the very earth itself was stained red for many months. Our brainwashing was complete. I ran through entire colonies hacking limbs, ripping hearts from chests, and putting heads on stakes. The air was filled with clouds of blood, fragments of exploded ribs; the ground littered with blue intestines leaking excrement, pieces of yellow spongy fat, rope-like tendons and chunks of twitching muscle. I disembowelled people, decapitated people, and skinned people alive. It was a massacre on a massive scale. Pure butchery.

"We were tricked into genocide. Kill the enemy, kill the humans responsible for destroying our race. We rioted like gods, revelling in our new-found freedom, exploring our powers. We dealt death and visited our wrath upon them.

"The Dehas saw humans as animals, no smarter than a chicken or a squirrel. We slaughtered them like food animals — and knew that they would kill us *if* they could. People were weaker, less intelligent and, as time passed, we cared less and less what we did with them. So, we hunted them, we butchered them, and we ate.

"Adults we put in clay kilns, potted and seasoned with wild garlic; children we gutted, stuffed with rosemary and mint, and roasted on spits.

"We laughed and killed and ate the stupid creatures we were told destroyed our kind.

"We laughed at their screams.

"We re-lived the false memories of our past — the seven — my love and me. We killed for years and years with no idea of the truth. The prison population dwindled, on the brink of eradication, despite record numbers coming to the planet. The Guardians were clueless, to begin with, but they eventually discovered Matheson and Brogan's deeds and brought them to the light, and to the attention of the Believers. They were tried and executed. This was a turning point for prison planet Earth, and for us. When we discovered the deceit of our foster parents — how they had manipulated and used us — we were devastated. How would you feel if you were to discover your real creators, your parents, were power-hungry sadistic murderers? That they chose to abuse their power and intellect to create real monsters — us! — and then sent them into the world to kill for fun.

"My love and I awoke from what we had done and felt deep shame and sincere remorse. We saw the truth and were forever changed by it. We were damaged by what we had done — the lives we had taken, the unspeakable horrors that we had perpetrated. To wake up one day and realise you are the real monster, and that the humans we killed were the real victims, was almost unbearable. We saw that — my love and I

— painful and world-shattering though it was. But the other five never awoke, refused to see, and they remain enslaved by the NTB illusions even now. They cannot believe that it was all an illusion — that they are the evil ones. It would be too much for them to bear.

"Soon after our awakening, Aurum and I found Idra.

"She had washed up on the north coast of the island, wearing a cadet uniform not too dissimilar from the one this poor soul was wearing —" here Talon pauses to gesture to the girl in the hammock. "She had been repeatedly raped and then left for dead by the worst of my dark family, Caelum the demiurge.

"Her story was just one of many similar cases happening all around the coast. Caelum and Gaudium, my brothers, started to see the humans as vessels to carry their seed and to build our ranks. They brought women to chambers deep inside the earth and subjected them to unspeakable acts. Kept in a place between life and death, a fearful realm of pain, after they had born children, the women were either discarded or eaten by their offspring.

"You know the power and intelligence Idra holds, Tommy, or, at least, have some idea. She used her powers to escape — through the sea of deformities that inhabit the deep tunnels of this island, she fought her way to freedom. I had helped dig most of those tunnels. They were based around old, disused service tunnels that the Guardians had once used to transport prisoners. At the very heart of those tunnels is the throne room, where the other Dehas dwell. I chose to reject their subterranean life, their life of false revenge — a lie of a life. With my love, I chose this life. We settled in the cliffs near the sea. I tunnelled, created more caves. And rather than slaughtering new prisoners, we helped them. We saw them as orphans, like us. Lost kin trying to find some peace. We helped as many as we could, took them to safety, and killed many Barrenites. We never left witnesses alive. But the evil under the land is ever growing, ever intensifying. The ramifying tunnels run deep, so deep I've forgotten just how far they stretch — but they are supported by the bones of the dead, bones and skulls.

"In the deep throne room sits their king, Caelum, seated on a throne of carved bone and marble, sealed with the blood of innocents. To him are brought sacrifices: people torn apart for his pleasure. In the same cave is the Dehas' round table — a huge black marble table, around which we created our laws. That cavern calls to me. As do my kin. Despite all my resistance, they keep calling to me in the insane labyrinths of my dreams. If I'm honest, there is a part of me that wants to be with them, and that urge only grows stronger the older I become. I itch to descend into those deep, hadean tunnels and reclaim my throne. To become what I am supposed to be. To trap light. I know it's unimaginable for you, Tommy, but part of me is pure evil — all it wants to do is kill. I fight this urge, this instinct, and imprison it afresh every single day."

Tommy stares at Talon as he strops his blade fingers together, making metallic *schink-schink* noises.

"And Aurum, Talon? How did she die?" Tommy asks with quiet curiosity.

"It was my brother Gaudium who ended my love's life. In a time, long ago, I considered Gaudium my closest ally," scoffs Talon.

"We were to be a new family of three, Aurum, Gaudium and I. We wanted to build our own clan and to try to redeem our past transgressions. It was not to be. She staggered from the woods one day with one of Gaudium's arrows lodged in her chest. I tried to pull the arrow out, but my blades accidently cut the arrow too close to her wound and I couldn't grip it with my fingers. I clamped the arrow in my teeth and pulled it out. I could taste her blood, sweet and perfumed. Aurum had been collecting herbs. I couldn't save her. I wasn't there for her when she needed me most. I will forever blame myself. No matter how fast I am, it's never fast enough. Fate always wins the race of life."

"I'm so sorry, Talon," Tommy says.

"The worst thing came next. I knew that Aurum was pregnant with our child and that the child was still alive inside Aurum as she lay dying. And so, I cut it out. I saved the baby, but in so doing, I had to further hurt my dying True Love. In the end, I killed Aurum to save our child," Talon says.

"Daria," Tommy whispers, with tears brimming in his eyes.

"Yes. My very own Angel."

"And then you killed Aurum's killer?"

"I left my Angel with Idra and Thankwell and hunted for three weeks until I finally found Gaudium. He was killing a small group of prisoners. They had no weapons and no idea what was going on. He was torturing one of them when I swept down upon him."

There was a lengthy silence as Talon drank. The silence was briefly broken once by a heart-felt sigh from Talon, then he resumed his drinking. Tommy waited a time for Talon to continue, but curiosity bubbling like Idra's tonic on the fossilised bone hearth, Tommy asks,

"How did you kill him?"

Talon thought awhile. "He just seemed to come apart in my hands."

"Good. He deserved to die for what he did."

"It felt like the right thing to do," Talon replies. "Later, I thought about how much he loved Aurum. My anger blinded me to the thought that such thing could have been anything other than murder. As he was dying, he tried to tell me it was an accident and that he was sorry."

"So, what was the truth?" asks Tommy.

"I couldn't say. I was too angry to find out. He just fell apart in my hands," Talon says, tears falling unashamedly from his eyes. "Let me tell you more."

"Okay, Talon. Please be calm, though. Don't be like me in the forest, or I might have to smash you back," Tommy says cheekily, wanting to lighten the mood more than anything.

"That would be unwise, young Astilla," says Talon, drinking more tonic. "I was known as Secretas," the demon continues. "There's a rhyme I remember from childhood. The seven of us used the rhyme to tease one another, in a light-hearted way; but we also used the words to hurt one another, when we felt mad. We never really understood what the words meant: 'One for sorrow, two for joy, three for a girl, four for a boy, five for silver, six for gold'; and I'm presuming I was 'seven for a secret never to be told.' Although, there was an alternate version of the rhyme and the doctors fused the two versions into one poem to give us our names. This version was: 'One for sorrow, two for mirth, three for a funeral, four for a birth, five for heaven, six for hell, seven's the Devil (his own self).' So, Matheson and Brogan fused two nursery rhymes to create a mutated verse which they then used to name their mutated offspring. Then they chose to name us in Latin, a long dead language, perhaps to add to our mystique or, perhaps — and I think this is more likely — because they were elitist, pompous arseholes. But, anyway, our names came about like this: 'One for sorrow,' Tristitia is derived from the Latin for *sad*; 'two for joy,' Gaudium is Latin for *the joy*; 'three for a funeral,' Funeralna comes from the Latin for *funeral*; 'four for a boy,' Puer is Latin for *boy* (although, Puer is *very* clearly a girl!); 'five for heaven,' Caelum is Latin for *heaven*; 'six for gold,' Aurum is Latin for *gold*; 'seven for a secret never to be told,' Secretas is Latin for *unknown*, a secret.

"Tristitia, Funeralna, Puer, and Aurum were the females; Gaudium, Caelum and I — 'the secret never to be told' — were the males. What more could we have known? A name said lovingly is simple to acknowledge. A name declared harshly is simple, too. We were not to blame for our hidden darkness. For a while, we were as all human children — children who wanted to obey the wishes of their parents and saw one another, not just as brothers and sisters, but as loving friends.

"At a far later date, in the cold chambers of the Guardians NTB learning pods, we were shown what we had done, what our parents had created, and what I had to acknowledge as our true label: laboratory-created abominations of Nature. After the execution of Matheson and Brogan, the Guardians gathered us up to console us. They tried to convince us that we were the result of loving experiments combining Brogan's innovative dream extraction with Matheson's knowledge of genetic engineering. But we didn't believe them. We had been lied to enough in our lives to recognise more of the same. I could see that I was the devil to those Guardians testing me at the compound. They tried to hide their revulsion, but I saw it plainly. To them, I was worse than Frankenstein's monster. He was a monster made from the amalgamation of dead human body parts, sewn together and then reanimated. He wasn't real, like us, though; he was just a story by the ancient author Mary Shelley. How I loved that story. I thought the monster a child. He was merely a flesh golem whereas I was the fusion of a thousand nightmares made flesh. Later in my life, I found human literature a great solace to me. For hundreds of years, I contemplated their diverse works. I devoured all I could find, but few words stuck with me like those I first read in *Frankenstein*: 'Did I request thee, maker, from my clay/ To mould me man, did I solicit thee/ From darkness to promote me?" These words — from John Milton's great poem *Paradise Lost* — rang true for me so many times. And, though my creators were far worse than Victor Frankenstein, I never wanted them dead. I neither thanked them nor condemned them. They were twisted individuals that wanted to be gods. They tried to control their creations, as every parent does to some degree. Children raised to chase unrealistic standards are ubiquitous. It seems a common theme in all families: you (the child) will be more than me (the parent).

"People don't necessarily fear truth — whether it be the truth behind their lives or the lies that are contained within this truth. People only fear the *unveiling*. They fear turning the rock over far more than those dark, squirming creatures that are hidden beneath the rock. I've had a long time to analyse my life, and now I'm content. With the help of my child and my friends, I have purged my brain of lies and the world seems a much less barren and cruel place.

"But my curse of longevity is to also say farewell to the ones that I have helped. When all light from my world is far away, it's the truth that keeps me stable.

"I was drawn out of my reality and imprisoned into this nightmare form against my will. I realise that I am to live on for some time, I may even live to see the Sun destroy the Earth, but when I die, I'll go back to my reality, back to the radiant Mandala," Talon lifts his head to drink the dregs of his tonic and sees the confusion in Tommy's eyes.

Tommy thinks Talon is probably drunk. His story made sense, for the most part, but seemed to jump about a bit and make less sense towards the end. Talon *had* drunk nearly all Idra's tonic.

"Would you like to see what I'm talking about?" says Talon suddenly.

And before Tommy can react, Talon's palm is on Tommy's forehead.

Tommy leaves everything he knows behind — his aching body, his fears, his hopes, his future, his past — and is transported from this agreed reality into something *other*.

He shoots through a portal in Talon's head and plunges into where Talon originated, to where all life had its origin. Tommy finds himself in a neon pool, pulsing with pure life-force. He is part of this force as it spans out — stretching and interconnecting, immeasurable and abundant — and its branches are everywhere. As it moves like a ghost through the multi-verse, Tommy clings to the energy. He wants to become one with this source energy. It feels like home. He feels like he belongs inside the radiant Mandala, the true Barbelo: *The Source.*

CHAPTER TEN
Belonging

Control your own destiny or someone else
will.

-Jack Welch-

10

Talon helps Tommy load provisions onto Slash for the remaining trip to the Forever Stairs — the huge and ancient concrete stairway which leads from the ocean to Tommy's final destination: the Lanes. Thankwell had given him a few pots of herbs and spices — *Seasoning makes food better*, the big man's voice booms in his memory — and three fresh whiting fish. Indra kindly donated some of her pipe herbs and a bottle of her famous tonic. Talon, who has given him so much already, gives only advice. The two of them are alone on a small quay, Tommy having already said his goodbyes to Idra and her giant son.

"Death follows a certain rule: don't follow, lead," he muses mysteriously. "Astilla is a good name for a leader of men. Perhaps you *can* change the lives of people there in the lanes for the better. But, Tommy, always remember what you saw on that cliff top and stay one mile from the coast. The Barrens belongs to those who live beneath. You have a chance at a normal life, amongst your own kind but, if anyone asks who you are, tell them you are Astilla, of the northern cliff coastal clan. I doubt the prisoners would respond well to the son of the person who banished them. Take care, young Tommy. You will be in our thoughts forever, my friend." And with this, Talon pushes Slash away from the quay's rickety, wooden jetty.

Talon's terrifying plate-bones glint in the moonlight. *His smile,* thinks Tommy. *What a horrendous parting sight.* Remembering Talon's tale of the rampage of the Dehas — imagining those flesh-rending jaws being the last thing a dying person sees — he supresses a shudder. He watches the spiky nightmare of Talon's silhouette walk along the rickety jetty and disappear into the darkness, as Slash sails into the night, disappearing into the gently rolling, moonlit waves.

Tommy sails westward, the vast ocean to one side and the terror of this island to the other. He feels the dark oceanic depths yawning beneath him, as silver-tinted clouds drift above him. Looking landwards, he thinks about the Barrens and its population of — *What did Talon call them?* — abominations. *Someplace under there are those rat-bastard believers — those hooded priests — their black souls as empty as the dark matter of space. We'll meet again. I promise it. And I'll make you pay for those cadets — for all your victims.*

Alone for the first time in a long while, he embraces the isolation and, between his sailing duties, his still tonic-delicate mind ponders the heavens: endless planets that rotate around in elliptical orbits, innumerable stars, and worlds to visit and explore. *Will I ever see another planet or another moon, another sun? There's so much to do and life is so short. Unless you're Talon, that is. If I could live as long as Talon, I wouldn't stay on one planet my entire life.*

Thinking of his long-lived friend, his mind turns back to Idra's cave and the wounded cadet recuperating there. *Should I have left her?* He wonders. Even though he knows the injured cadet is in the safest place she can be — as safe as one can be on this Barrenite-riddled isle — he cannot shake a feeling of concern for her. *No, this feeling is stronger than concern. Love? No. Pity?* He remembers her as he had found her: her pale face, spattered with blood, mutilated bodies and gore and shit surrounding her. *Maybe I pity her, but mostly I'm sorry. Sorry she was so helpless, sorry for her pain, sorry I couldn't save the others. All I can offer you is protection, of sorts, and a doorway to revenge. You can step through it if you wish, the choice is yours. We always have a choice. Don't we?*

The sea was obligingly calm throughout his voyage and Tommy sailed almost in a daze, only roused from his thoughts by the sight of a precipitous cliff growing on the horizon. As he draws nearer, the regular zigzag of stairs, like a small tattoo on the cliff surface, just starts to become visible. The cliff slowly fills his whole vision and the small stairs become mid-sized and then vast. A small jetty of indeterminate age, with missing boards and seaweed- and barnacle-encrusted piles, also appears.

Tommy cannot help but think about his future in the Lanes. *Will this be the place I meet my contemporaries? A place where like-minded folk tussle with philosophical and scientific issues: the micro and the macro, infinity and nothingness?*

He smiles a broad, mildly insane, smile — a smile to rival Talon's unusual grin. Maybe not as scary; maybe more so. It is a grin filled with both sorrow and hope, in a young but heavily scarred face, framed with long feral hair, which whips around in the sea breeze. With cold blue eyes he studies the steps.

The ancient steps of the western cliff face stretch far into the sky. The upper stretches of the stairs are shrouded in clouds. After almost twelve hours of sailing, it looks daunting to Tommy. Despite his strong urge to being amongst people, he has a stronger urge for sleep. As well as the long sail, his head still ached somewhat from Idra's Tonic. He knew he would benefit from sleep before attempting to scale the vertiginous Forever Stairs. Knotting Slash onto the least rotten wooden cleats on the jetty, as Thankwell had taught him, he takes down and stores Slash's sails. Uncertain as to how long the catamaran will stay here, he secures the boat as thoroughly as he can. Standing back, admiring his handywork, Tommy thinks the only way Slash will be lost now is if a storm rips the dilapidated jetty from the stairs. Making his way over the slippery, slime-coated jetty, and the massive concrete base of the stairs, he starts to ascend. After maybe half an hour of climbing, he reaches a large mezzanine platform where the stairs change direction. He makes a tent with his joining tools and pitches it as near to the cliff face as he can. *Don't want to roll off the platform in my sleep.*

Tommy finds some driftwood further up the staircase, *Perfect*, he thinks. He builds a fire in front the tent, just the way Talon had shown him. *At least, if I do roll out of my tent, the fire will wake me up before I roll off the edge. Burns are no fun, but they're better than falling to your death.*

As he warms himself by his fire, he takes a few gulps of Idra's Tonic. He stares into the flames and, caught in a trance by the bewitching dancing plasma, he thinks of Talon's story, he thinks about his mother and father, he thinks about quantum theory and the entanglement of particles. His mind flits from subject to subject like the dancing lights in his campfire. He thinks about the place where Talon is from, about portals, about the nameless injured cadet, he also thinks, rather graphically and gruesomely — *Damn my vivid imagination!* — about Thankwell biting someone in half.

Managing to drag himself away from his tired and wandering thoughts, he cooks one of Thankwell's whiting over the fire. Sipping some of Idra's Tonic, as the fish sizzles, he feels that the tonic is having a milder effect on him this time. It warms him, taking the pain from behind his eyes and wiping the sadness of his journey from his mind — banishing thoughts of blood and bodies and death.

Then Tommy has an epiphany. His subconscious mind, always working problems in the background, visualises a unified form and brings it to the foreground. It is a familiar pattern — the one he used to create the joining tools and the EPC. His new theories on quantum physics all form patterns, like the patterns of numbers, like patterns of fractals. The pattern is a radiant mandala of thought stretching out across the universe, connecting all the stars — a mycelium network with fungal spores — a dark matter pattern of similar structure filling the universe with stars and planets sprouting on it like fruiting bodies. The pattern is like interconnected coral reefs, neural networks in the mind, like the lines on the back of a person's hand — crisscrossing back and forth — and, at the nodes, hairs grow, or planets or corals or stars. He sees the pattern of life, of reality. It is clear and supremely calming.

Anything is possible now, thinks Tommy. He climbs inside his tent and, to the random pops of his fire and the metronomic sound of lapping waves, slides into a deep sleep.

Not knowing for how long he slept, all notion of time lost, Tommy starts to climb the steps in darkness and, as he reaches the top step of the Forever Stairs, the sun is just rising. Catching his breath, Tommy looks at the perfect morning sky: lavenders layered with peach, pastel green flecks, and the hidden fire of the sun raising sharper hues, heavenly highlights.

Turning from the dazzling vista, he saw the large, fortified wall of the Lanes not far from him. It was huge — almost as high as the Forever Stairs. *It must be one hundred an' fifty feet if it's a yard!* thinks Tommy. *Oh, well — another job for my grappling hook.*

Upon scaling the fortified wall with little difficulty, Tommy's thoughts briefly turn to what Talon had told him about the Barrenites not attacking near the sea. *If scaling this wall was no problem for me, those monsters would fly up it! And yet, because it is close to the sea, they refuse to do so. Strange. I wonder how far exactly from the sea they feel safe? And how would they know? Further, what is it about the sea that scares them, anyway? Are they afraid of curious squid? Belligerent crabs? A mildly irate herring? It's stupid. Real underground monsters fearing some mythical sea god. It's more than stupid — it's preposterous!*

Plopping himself gracelessly down, his legs swinging over on the Lane-side edge of the wall, Tommy is fascinated by what stretches out before him.

He can see the wall upon which he is sitting tracing an elongated oval shape, which disappears into the far distance. In the shadow of the wall, clinging to it, almost a mile thick, is a band of multi-coloured, eclectic dwellings. In front of the houses, colourful plots of crops reach inwards towards the centre of the Lanes, each plot demarcated by makeshift boundaries of metal, driftwood, plastics and wire. The entire view, from this vantage-point, has a dizzying effect on Tommy. And, focusing on the small shapes of people that he can see wandering in and around these plots of land he thinks, *I'm no longer alone. This is a new beginning for me, just like the one I dreamt of when I was trapped in the Facility. I can live with these industrious people, find like-minded individuals and finally start living my* real *life.*

Tommy's eyes darted from one curious house to the next, soaking up the strange sights and sounds. Sounds rise and fall like the sea. He hears distant singing, drum beats over shouting voices and the distant whisper of the sea. Something sweet smelling comes to him on the air, something sugary, and he hungrily scans below for the source. Unable to determine where the lovely smell comes from, he looks out over the particoloured shacks, the occasional chimney jutting out like a pipe from an old man's mouth. Here and there little plumes of smoke drift as people cook their food. His stomach rumbles and he wonders what delights these strange folks are cooking? What delicate cuisines? From somewhere, Tommy picks out the faint sound of snoring, thankfully nothing like Thankwell's racket. The noises of the Lanes make a strange symphony, one which his engineering mind compares to the unoiled cogs of a mighty machine, creaking in unison.

Looking into the distance now, over this bustling community, as the morning haze lifts, he can just make out a single building at the centre of the farming land. Most of the noise seems to be coming from that direction.

Tommy decides that heading to that building is as good a goal as anything. Looking at the wall below, there is no obvious pathway down, so he decides to walk along the top of the wall for a distance to see if anything turns up.

Tommy walks almost three miles along the considerable wall's circumference, until the straight-line distance to the building in the centre seems the shortest. As he walks, he also notices a strip of houses that stretches from the wall to the centre of the lanes, a peninsula of shacks, like a solitary spoke of a wheel.

Looking around below him, Tommy spots a small cabin, next to the wall, and, using his grappling hook, descends into the seemingly disused hut. Standing behind the small hut he notices a strong smell emanating from it. *Just great! I'm standing behind a shithouse! Lovely. So much for fresh sea air.* He chuckles to himself and a quick look around makes it clear that the only way out of where he is, aside from climbing, is to go through someone's house.

His joining tools and the EPC goes into Tommy's bag before he decides to clamber through a beaded curtain and into someone's bedroom or living room. He peeks through the beaded curtain wall and is relieved to see that no one is home. There are the glowing embers of a fire in a brass fireplace, a wooden floor, and, to the right, is a small bed, with framed pictures over it. The shack is about one hundred and sixty square feet and most of this area is covered in a red, shag-pile rug, which has clearly seen better days. Above the fire is a large mirror set in an ornate, gold frame. *That looks like it belongs in a Space Museum*, Tommy thinks. To the left of the mirror, on the floor, is a solid looking cast-iron safe, with a large golden wheel in its centre. The weight of the safe had warped the floorboards beneath it and it occupies an obvious indentation.

Tommy takes a few deep breaths and then bolts for the door at the other side of the shack. He pauses briefly at the doorway and then, out into the Lanes he goes.

The Lanes are named for the tunnel-like passageways which messily wind between the small, closely packed houses. The networks of criss-crossing pathways are formed naturally by the footfalls of generations of prisoners that had survived the Barrens and made it to this oasis of hope.

Tommy winds his way through alien sights and an assortment of smells, which range from spiced heaven to aged latrine stench, and tries to keep in a straight line towards his destination — well, as straight as he can manage in the twisting, narrow lanes of the Lanes. The kaleidoscopic, random arrangements of colours are shocking to his senses after sixteen years in the sterile environment of the Drumcroon facility.

Tommy can hardly keep his eyes focused on where he is going as one intriguing scene upon another unfolds before him. However, he does find the absence of people somewhat disturbing.

Tommy follows his ears, the music getting louder and louder. Drums and singing, laughing, guitars, and the sound of a solitary flute rise from what he could only presume to be the nucleus of this visually exciting labyrinthine system. Emerging from yet another narrow street, distracted by an unusual structure, he finds himself tumbling face-first into the dirt. He wipes the earth from his eyes and sees, outstretched in front of him, a long green glove. His eyes flick upwards to see a frowning young woman with striking red hair, before she roughly grabs him by the scruff of his neck and drags him off a prostrate figure in the mud.

"Clumsy wee shite! You're on my mother!" she says.

Mumbling his apologies, Tommy looks around to see staggering, dirt-covered people, some wallowing, like clothed pigs, in the mud. *Are they all drunk?* There are several fights taking place that, at first, Tommy mistakes for people hugging.

Tommy helps the young redhead get her bedraggled, disoriented mother to her feet.

"I'm Marie-Ann O'Shea; and you must be new. Come on, let me get you a drink, I'm running the risk of sobriety myself, if you catch my drift!"

"I'm Tommy Sa— Shit!" Marie-Ann bolts off holding Tommy's hand, almost dislocating his shoulder. "Come on then, Tommy Shit," she says. Tommy, dragging behind her, is unable to see her smile. She pulls him through the crowds and towards the building at the centre of this strange theatre of drunken fools. Now and again, drunks paw at Tommy's now dirty face and laugh. One drunk pinches Marie-Ann O'Shea's arse. She stops suddenly. Tommy crashes into her from behind, winding himself slightly as her shoulder jabs into his solar plexus. She stares at the prurient drunk who is now leering at her. She kicks him smartly in the shin and, as he hops around holding his leg and cursing, she pushes him over.

"You filthy little wasp!" Marie-Ann shouts over her shoulder, dragging Tommy back into her wake. She looks back to Tommy occasionally, smiling as she pushes through the crowd, and Tommy returns her smile. *She's a force of nature,* thinks Tommy, as she smashes into one drunk after another, knocking them over into the well-trodden earth, laughing as they shout and slur undignified blasphemies after her. Tommy watches the developing trail of destruction she leaves behind her with amusement.

Arriving at the three-tiered *Weeping Willow* pub, Tommy laughs a full, uncontrollable laugh at the woman's antics. Marie-Ann had hoofed another drunk out of her path. This man had landed face-first into a plump woman's breasts. His pale, porcine face had time to contort into a surprised, happy look before the well-endowed woman smashed a bottle over his bald head.

Kicking through the saloon doors, Marie-Ann looks towards a man at the end of the bar who is cleaning a silver flute while puffing on an orange-coloured, pineapple-shaped pipe. Marie-Ann's father stops his polishing, removes his pipe and a smile starts to form. But, upon spying the boy she was with, the smile dies on his lips and he returns to polishing and pipe-chugging with a frown firmly fixed on his face.

Tommy stares around the bar through eyes still stinging a little from the mud. The pub was reminiscent of images of Old Earth — an ancient New Orleans blues bar from sometime in the distant past. It was well known that appropriate architecture and interior design can have a calming effect. Tommy remembered this from some old scientific papers he had read, perhaps when he was eight. This building, he remembered, had been a lasting present from the Guardians to the prisoners. It was to give some level of comfort to ease their troubled existence.

Until now, *The Weeping Willow* had been folklore to Tommy. He had overheard prisoners talking about it during their processing at Drumcroon. Tommy had pieced together passing comments and, over the years, had formed a history of what the prisoners called The Last Pub on Earth.

The Weeping Willow was ostensibly built as a meeting place, like a town hall, a safe place where prisoners could talk through their issues in a calming atmosphere. It was a stately building, but years and years of renovations had rendered it disjointed. Repairs were made with whatever materials the prisoners could salvage, and styles became mixed and confused. Originally it had one floor but, at some point, two other rickety, wooden levels were added. These additional floors originally accommodated the more vulnerable prisoners — the infirm and the ill — or were used by honeymooning couples. The building was, both then and now, the hub of the prisoner's social and political structure.

It seemed to Tommy to be merely a bustling pub, like in the stories of pre-Dagon Earth, serving fermented goods at a blistering pace. A place of warmth and good cheer, comradery and community. What Tommy did not know, at this point, was that a deadly virus was at work in the Lanes.

It had come, like many viruses do, from nowhere. It was quickly transmitted, there was no cure, and it was certain death, often in less than two weeks (although those two weeks were a painful eternity to the afflicted.) Many of the population who showed symptoms, and had seen the disease in its final stages, opted for suicide rather than go through that living nightmare. The virus effecting the very old and very young first, mothers killed their offspring, children killed their parents, and death pacts were commonplace. The virus decimated the Lanes, and the settlement might have perished had the prisoners not discovered something. It was first noticed, some years before the arrival of the young Tommy Salem that, although there was no cure for the virus, alcoholics rarely died from it. They might catch it, but their deaths were from suicide or alcohol-linked morbidities. The virus did not kill them. It was hypothesized that the virus was minutely sensitive to the small levels of alcohol circulating in a drunk person's blood. This alcohol did not totally kill the virus — a drunk deprived of booze inevitably died from it — but it stopped the progression of the disease, and its horrific symptoms. Alcohol, although not a cure, was a life support machine — a stasis pod which kept people from the painful later stages.

Understandably this gave the prisoners a taste for alcohol, mostly in copious quantities. Alcohol had become not just an occasional escape from reality but a necessary and daily source of survival.

It was the Dionysus virus which had changed the use of the Guardians' building. *The Weeping Willow* pub was now a drunken congregation of prisoners wanting to get as wasted as possible to survive. The Guardians would have abominated what had happened to their hall, had they known about it, but contact between the Lanes and the Guardians had become increasingly sporadic.

In years gone by, the Guardians would move supplies into the Lanes via a large supply tunnel. Since the emergence of the deadly Dionysus virus, to minimise contact, the Guardians simply air-dropped the supplies. For safety reasons — *their* safety! — the Guardians collapsed the main supply tunnel. As the fishing boats, donated by the Guardians for the prisoners to fish the seas, were, over time, dismantled and used to create, or strengthen, buildings, the Lanes became less self-sufficient, increasingly more dependent on the Guardian air drops.

When the prisoners requested distillation apparatus, ready-to-drink spirits and alcohol of all types, the Guardians grudgingly acceded. Observing the virus whittling away the population of the Lanes, the Guardians saw each of the monthly drops as the last meal of condemned inmates. It is instinctual to the humanitarian side of people to want to make the sick and dying as peaceful as they can. Yet, slowly, the population of the Lanes recovered — and incoming prisoners did not die as quickly as projected. The Guardians just assumed the recovery showed that the virus had run its course, or the inmate's immune systems had adapted — but the virus lived. The virus was still running rampant in the Lanes.

"Jonesy!" Marie-Ann shouts, leaning over the bar, smiling and flicking her long hair like she had not a care in the world. "A couple of specials for me and my new drinking buddy."

"Aye, Right-O, Marie-Ann. Coming right up." This came from a gnarled, thinly built man in his late thirties. Lip curled up at one side, revealing some charred stumps of teeth, he looked Tommy up and down as he approached.

"Who's this shower of shite!" says Jonesy in what Tommy could not know is a thick, Belfast accent. "And what the fuck are you looking at, sunshine?"

Tommy looks away, shrugging, trying not to further irritate the volatile dark-haired man who is now starting to smile at Marie-Ann.

"Leave him alone, Jonesy!" Marie-Ann smiles. "Yer full of it! He tripped over me ma, and now he's covered in what ye jabber. So... get them drinks."

He grins at Marie-Ann and shoots another frown towards Tommy. Under Jonesy's skin, at his temples, black swirls briefly appear and then flee, like two deep sea squid disappearing back into the depths. *Trick of the light*, thinks Tommy and tries to diffuse the situation.

"I'm Tommy," he says. "Sorry for tramping mud into your bar, Jonesy."

Jonesy's smiles at the idea that it is his bar and, tension diffused somewhat, Tommy does not think any more of those dark shifting shapes he saw under the bartender's face.

Jonesy stops making the drinks, runs a bar towel under a cold tap and throws it in his face. "You must be new, Tommy. Here. Clean yourself up."

"You're such a grumpy fucker, Jonesy!" says Marie-Ann shaking her head.

"He doesn't need a fucking towel — he needs a dunk in the fucking sea!" Jonesy says.

"Where the fuck are those specials!" Marie-Ann mugs in a bad impression of Jonesy's coarse accent.

"Are ya sure he can handle it? He looks like one of Bowdon's farts would knock him out?" Jonesy says, nodding over to a person who could only be Bowdon. At the end of the bar, Bowden tries to oblige Jonesy with a fart, but can only wetly shit himself.

"Och, Bowden! You fucking dirty bastard! Get out!" Jonesy points to the door and Bowdon despondently squelches past Tommy and Marie-Ann, head down. As he passes by, Marie-Ann and Tommy were treated to a blast of the foul scent, which made them both heave and then laugh.

Then Marie-Ann looks at Tommy, scrutinising him carefully.

"Would you look at that, now," Marie-Ann says quietly, her green elbow-length glove caressing the side of young Tommy's left cheek where he had wiped most of the mud away.

"Is there something wrong?" Tommy asks worriedly.

"There you are, Tommy boy," says Marie-Ann. She smiles the sweetest of smiles and Tommy cannot help but return the strange searching stare, his heart swelling strangely in his chest. The moment is ruined by the mangy barkeep who slams down their drinks on the counter right in front of them, some of the foaming contents slopping over the sides.

"Would you look at this, Jonesy," says Marie-Ann, still staring at Tommy's face. "No black veins in sight."

"Bollocks! He's probably covered in them from the neck down."

Marie-Ann grabs both wooden tankards, full of a frothing and slightly fizzing drink, and then primly says to Jonesy: "Well, I might just enjoy finding that out."

She marches off to find a table near the window, leaving Tommy staring at Jonesy with an idiot grin on his face. Jonesy's black swirls start to surface again.

"I'll — I'll just ..." Tommy mumbles, pointing in the direction of Marie-Ann's fast disappearing back.

"Fucking eeedjit!" Jonesy barks as Tommy turns to start navigating the milling drunks of *The Weeping Willow*.

He finds Marie-Ann near the saloon doors, at a table for two, staring out the window. *Maybe keeping an eye out for her mother*, Tommy thinks.

Approaching slowly, he could see Marie-Ann's attention is on the rain as it starts to speckle the window, and then begins to lash into the pane. The sight of Marie-Ann at that window seemed to morph into an old oil painting, in his romanticised mind. Perhaps one from the ancient Impressionist period. He thinks the title of this painting would have been: *The Storm*. A curious feeling settles over him as he places himself across from her on an old wooden stool — a feeling of *déjà vu*, that he had been here before. He stares at Marie-Ann, smiling at her, trying to act normal and remembers what Talon had said about sticking to your path in life. That advice feels perfect as he smiles at Marie-Ann, searching her bright but troubled eyes. Marie-Ann pushes the tankard over to Tommy across the stained wooden table.

"Welcome to *The Weeping Willow*, Tommy Boy, and the end of the world." She turns her attention briefly from Tommy to the falling rain and assorted drunks outside, sighs a little and then returns his gaze and raises her tankard as if in a toast.

"Eternal happy hour awaits," she says and gulps at the fizzy liquid.

Tommy repeats the toast and drinks, feeling compelled to match the drinking speed of this lady. He immediately regrets this decision as he feels the fluid burning down his throat and setting fire to his stomach. He powers through the pain, gulping at the beverage, all the while cursing his competitive nature. The drinks finished, they slam their tankards down. Marie-Ann smiles and looks at Tommy as if waiting for something. His face slowly screws up and he slaps his hand over his mouth, as if to stop flames bursting out.

"What do you think of that, Tommy Boy?" Marie-Ann asks, noticing his pale, sweat-beaded brow.

"What the fuck was *that*!" Tommy mumbles through his hand — his eyes watering, his vision hazy and impaired. The hand not holding the tankard moves from vice-like grip of his mouth to rub at his throat. The brew had dried out his throat and, instead of quenching his thirst, it made him feel thirstier. Through his murky tear-filled eyes, he blinks at Marie-Ann. As the tears retreat into his tear ducts, Marie-Ann's neck and face start to swarm with moving black tentacles. They pulsate and move, getting darker and darker, before slowly fading back into her fair complexion. Tommy automatically leaps back away from Marie-Ann in his shock. His ears have a loud ringing in them, he cannot hear what she is saying to him. He also wonders why she is gesticulating towards him so frantically.

Tommy backs away from the still silently gesturing Marie-Ann ... and into Jung Heindricht.

Heindricht is a barbarian who thinks arguments are for people who cannot punch. At first, Tommy thinks he has backed into a wall. His ears still ringing, he feels the wall vibrating on his back, like it is growling. *Yes, that's it,* thinks Tommy surreally. *The wall behind me is growling.* Tommy spins around to be confronted by a wall of leather and black chest-hair. He looks further up to see Heindricht frowning down at him.

"Stupid boy!" spits the dark face of Heindricht through long, crooked teeth. Marie-Ann sees the punch before Heindricht throws it and leaps over the table. She throws one of the wooden tankards into Heindricht's angry face, to distract him, as she is moving, then pushes Tommy aside, before sending Heindricht reeling with a quick knee to the crotch. Jonesy drags Heindricht from the floor in a headlock and out of the bar.

"You're barred, Heindricht! Just for today, mind," Jonesy says as he reaches the wooden saloon doors. Then, using Heindricht's head to open the swinging doors, Jonesy sends him sprawling in the mud with a pushing kick to the posterior of the bent-over troublemaker. Heindricht stays where he is for a good five minutes — Tommy watches him nervously through the window — before starting his long crawl home, no doubt to nurse his embarrassing injury.

In that ball-shattering moment, Tommy's life changes. When that poor Neanderthal drunk fell — writhing in agony — on to the floor; Tommy fell in love.

(In the future, Tommy will poetically muse about this moment, thinking: *It was a cruel, drunk, intergalactic goblin who stole cupid's bow that day and peppered my heart with a quiver of love for a flame-haired barroom brawler.*)

As love blurs the lines between reality and romanticism, causing the dumbstruck few to act irrationally, problematically, painfully, he realises he has no plan for this. Tommy, for once, is without a plan. Planless. The supremely neat and organised schedule of his mind is thrown into chaos by the sight of an angel and the intoxication of raging hormones. No plan; just love. Something he has read about but never personally experienced. Until now. How far will he go for her? What will he get for her? Easy. He will go anywhere for her and get her everything she wants: everything that heaven and hell holds. Anything. He will tear this reality apart and drag into existence a world that she deserves. He will sacrifice himself for her. His heart now belongs to her. Somehow, it always has.

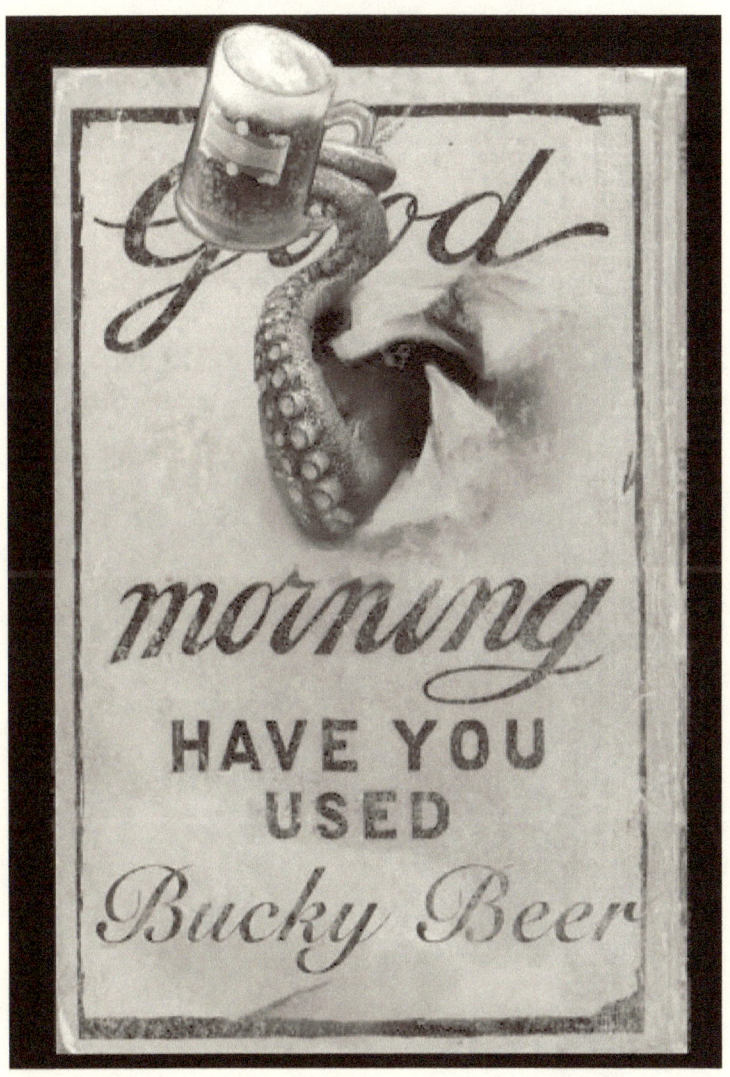

Don't miss out!

Visit the website below and you can sign up to receive emails whenever Wayne Hill publishes a new book. There's no charge and no obligation.

https://books2read.com/r/B-A-ERTO-PAUOB

BOOKS 2 READ

Connecting independent readers to independent writers.

Also by Wayne Hill

Splinter Salem
Splinter Salem Part One
Splinter Salem Part Two
Splinter Salem Part Three

www.ingramcontent.com/pod-product-compliance
Lightning Source LLC
Chambersburg PA
CBHW021106130626
46554CB00002B/553